Le Club d'Esclavage

At the Dungeon Master's Hand - Natalie Buchanan has been working non-stop for six weeks. Determined to enjoy a rare weekend off, she winds up at the mysterious Le Club d'Esclavage.

A Toy For Two - Megan Washington is the perfect daughter...as long as she keeps her wild streak hidden. Only after a trip to the Le Club d'Esclavage does she give free reign to her sexually adventurous spirit.

Yes, My Mistress - Dani Miller is the kind of girl who does her best to make everyone happy. She helps her parents out at their diner, she helps remind her friends to laugh, and she's always ready to take orders from her customers. When it's her turn to give the orders, the hunky bouncer at Le Club E'sclavage is just the man to follow her.

Le Club

D'Esclavage

At the Dungeon Master's Hand A Toy For Two Yes, My Mistress

By

Jennifer Cole

Lyrical Press, Inc.

New York

LYRICAL PRESS, INCORPORATED

Le Club d'Esclavage
10 Digit ISBN: 1-61650-144-8
13 Digit ISBN: 978-1-61650-144-0
Copyright © 2009, Jennifer Cole
Edited by Stephanie McGrath and Pamela Tyner
Book design by Renee Rocco
Cover Art by Renee Rocco

Lyrical Press, Incorporated
337 Katan Avenue
Staten Island, New York 10308
http://www.lyricalpress.com

PUBLISHER'S NOTE:
This book is a work of fiction. The names, characters, places, and incidents are products of the writer's imagination or have been used fictitiously and are not to be construed as real. Any resemblance to persons, living or dead, actual events, locale or organizations is entirely coincidental.

The publisher does not have any control over and does not assume any responsibility for author or third-party Web sites or their content.

Published in the United States of America by Lyrical Press, Incorporated
First Lyrical Press, Inc print publication: March 2010

DEDICATION

To my husband, Troy, for the countless times you sacrifice our together time, to allow me to indulge in my passion. I know it isn't easy.

At the Dungeon

Master's Hand

CHAPTER 1

Natalie sat with her two best friends in the back seat of the taxi. She'd tuned out their mindless chit-chat blocks ago and now watched the bright streetlights whiz by. The pleasant, cool night air of late September teased her skin through the open windows.

As a copy editor, she'd been working twenty-four-seven with the magazine's newest client, preparing an expansive layout feature for the next issue. A lot was riding on the spread. If successful, this project would be a huge stepping-stone in her career. Since Midge Patterson's retirement three months prior, Natalie'd had her eye on the unfilled copy chief's position and, come hell or high water, was determined to make it hers. She'd been biding her time and had proven herself more than capable in her four years with the highly successful magazine.

This was her first weekend off in six weeks and now, Natalie really needed to let loose. She intended to make the most of it. Having been cooped up in her office for so long, she'd almost forgotten there was a big old world outside the confines of those four, cell-block-grey walls. Truly, she would have liked nothing better than to be at home tonight, curled up in the corner of her cozy sofa, finishing off the romance novel she'd started more than a month ago. Or watching the *M*A*S*H* series she'd purchased on DVD three months ago, and had yet to open.

But, oh no, she'd allowed Megan and Dani to drag her out to God knows where, to do God knows what. She loved her two best friends with all her heart. The trio had known each other since first grade, and now, after her parents' passing four years earlier, they were the only family Natalie had left. After twenty-three years, she trusted them with her life, although considering some of the messes they'd dragged her into, she wasn't sure why.

Natalie was the sensible, levelheaded one in their trio. She'd had to study hard for good grades, worked several part-time jobs to put herself through college, and dedicated every spare moment to her career. Executive editor was definitely in her future.

Despite coming from old money, Megan was thrifty, organized and focused. She managed a trendy clothing store in a popular mall, primarily to feed her shopping addiction. As a clothes-horse, Megan couldn't pass up the employee discount, even though she could afford to pay three times the price for the products. With a politician father, parties were the norm of her everyday life, and good times hummed in her blood. Megan was always 'game on' in the name and pursuit of 'fun'.

Dani was a stereotypical blond, which would be fitting if she weren't a brunette. She was fun-loving, naïve, and innocent to a fault. Her family didn't have the money for Dani go to school, so she worked the day shift at her parents' local coffee shop. She loved her job and her customers adored her.

With Megan's lust for adventure and all things odd, and Dani's natural instincts to follow Megan's lead, it never failed the three would generally find themselves somewhere 'weird' and usually in trouble. And Natalie knew tonight would be no exception.

"Okay, Meg." Natalie finally broke into their conversation. "Where are you taking me?"

Her friends giggled excitedly.

Dani reached over, grabbed her hand, and gently kissed the back of it. "Nat, you really need to take a load off. You're going to get all wrinkly before you're thirty if you don't let go of all that stress."

Megan was still giggling beside her. "Dani's right, Nat. Now that the Marsden project is finished and on its way to print, it's time you let those gorgeous curls down and cut loose! Hell, we haven't spent any time with you since you were assigned that account. So tonight, you are ours."

"Well, for a little while anyway." Dani wagged her brows.

"What the hell is that supposed to mean?" Natalie asked nervously, glancing from one to the other. "Oh God, what are the two of you dragging me into?"

Neither one answered.

[11]

Megan and Dani resumed their chatter and Natalie once again tuned them out, wishing she were sitting in her apartment, enjoying complete silence and working her way through a bottle of red wine.

* * * *

From the window he watched the growing crowd below.

Initially he'd opened the club as a lark, just to stir up shit at City Hall. He honestly never thought he'd be issued a permit to open a BDSM club within the stuffy city limits. Once he had the permit in his hands, he'd worked day and night, opening Le Club d'Esclavage within four weeks, nearly a month ahead of schedule.

As he remembered the uproar the grand opening had caused, he didn't try to stop his lips from curling in amusement, especially since, as the owner, he had no desire to be in the public eye. His best friend Troy, a well-established and experienced Dom, had the ability to manipulate the media and maintain the position as front man of the operation.

Its appeal lay in being 'new,' so he'd expected the club to do well in the beginning, as an attraction for the curious, of course. However, he had no idea it would still be considered the place to be a year later. He felt bad for the owners of the three mainstream nightclubs who had closed their doors due to the lack of patronage. Every week his clientele increased to the point they had to start taking reservations for the private playrooms on the second floor.

The club generated more money than he'd ever imagined,

however, he had no need for it. Once the employees' wages and the day-to-day operating expenses were paid, whatever was left went to local charities. Anonymously.

* * * *

"We're here!" Megan and Dani squealed in unison.

Natalie, who hadn't been paying attention, looked out the window at a lengthy queue. Climbing out of the taxi she glanced up at the neon sign and gasped.

"Oh...my...God," she finally said. "We are *not* going in there." She stood shaking her head, gaping at her two friends giggling beside her.

"Damn straight," Megan replied as they each linked their arms with Natalie's and headed for the front door, bypassing those waiting in line.

* * * *

He tipped his bottle, taking the last pull off his beer as a yellow taxi stopped out front. Swallowing the pilsner, he watched the back door open. He recognized Dani Miller as she emerged from the passenger side accompanied by Megan Washington.

His heart rate quickened and his cock stirred restlessly inside his Dockers. *Could it be?* he wondered. No, that would be too good to be true. Although it would appear he had horseshoes up his ass when it came to success, even he couldn't possibly be this fucking lucky.

Holding his breath, he watched as one leg emerged from the passenger's side, and then a second. The creamy skin of her bare thighs, a tan suede mini-skirt, and then strawberry blond curls pulled back in a hair clip. He watched her stand and gawk open mouthed at the neon sign over the door. The look of stunned surprise on her pretty face made his balls pull up tight against his body.

"My God, she's here. She's really here," he said to the empty room. His grin of ardor broadened as he watched her two friends link arms with her, leading her through the front door, right into his domain.

Adjusting the thickening flesh between his legs, he smiled broadly in anticipation.

॥ ‖ ⁙ ⁞

"Hi, Mikey," Dani tipped her head coyly, greeting the man at the door.

"Good evening, ladies. Welcome to Le Club d'Esclavage," he greeted the threesome and winked at Dani.

Natalie spun her head around to look at a moony-eyed Dani and stifled another gasp. "Dani, have you..."

"Maybe once or twice," Dani snickered. "Now, come on, let's get in there."

Dani pulled them through the door Mikey held open. He stopped them short as they made their entrance. "I'll meet you shortly." He smiled at Dani as she giggled.

Natalie threw a speculative glance at her friend. How was it that after twenty-three years of sharing absolutely everything, she had no idea her friend was into the BDSM scene?

Le Club d'Esclavage was the newest sensation to hit their city. Roughly translated as 'The Club of Slavery,' it had turned the entire community on its ear when its grand opening a year ago had attracted record numbers of patrons from the surrounding areas. Le Club d'Esclavage was a scrupulously monitored establishment catering to adults interested in the BDSM scene. Whether you were a novice interested in participating in a little 'slap-and-tickle,' or a 'whip-me-beat-me-call-me-trash' hardcore enthusiast, Le Club d'Esclavage offered something to whet any appetite.

The owner of the club remained a mystery. His or her identity had never been revealed and all media correspondence regarding the popular establishment was conducted through its manager, Troy Simon. Troy was a vigilant observer and demanded all guests and employees follow the strict and necessary guidelines while patronizing the club. All arrangements of play must be consensual, no bestiality, no pain infliction for the sake of inflicting pain, no blood play, all engaging partners must practice safe play at all times. And above all else, have a great fucking time! It's just sex, after all.

During the grand opening of Le Club d'Esclavage, Troy was quoted as saying, "The owner would like to make one thing very clear. When you cross the threshold into Le Club d'Esclavage, it is your desire to participate completely in our manner of play, and such will be expected of you."

A shiver coursed through Natalie as she remembered editing that specific piece on the club from one of the reporters for her magazine. *In the Know* had been the only print media given an exclusive. Until then, she'd known nothing of the BDSM scene and had found herself mildly intrigued at the concept of pleasurable pain and domination and submission. However, she wasn't curious enough to give it a try.

Here she was, standing at the bar in the very club that had inspired numerous nights of naughty dreams and many mornings of damp panties. *Jesus*, she thought as she watched Megan order their drinks, *why in the* hell *do I continue to let her drag me into these situations?*

Loud dance music vibrated from the multiple speakers throughout the enormous room. Natalie sighed as she surveyed the growing crowd inside the dimly lit club. Oh how she longed to be alone in her quiet apartment.

The inside looked like every other night club she'd ever been in, except most of the patrons in Le Club d'Esclavage were dressed, or rather not dressed, in barely-there leather straps wrapping this way and that. Women wore bustiers pushing their naked breasts up and out for everyone's viewing pleasure. Many of the men wore leather pants with the seat missing, showing off ass cheeks of all sizes, or some type of pouch encasing their genitals. Bodies were bumping and grinding against one another on the dance floor. Couples, males with females, males with males, females with females, and a few threesomes she could see, were kissing, stroking and rubbing each other.

Natalie shivered at the erotic exchanges. In an attempt to tamp her growing arousal she emptied her glass and ordered a second fruity umbrella drink, this time with a double shot of rum.

It was going to be a very long night.

* * * *

Dani had disappeared half an hour earlier with Mikey, the doorman. Studying Megan, Natalie could clearly read her friend's mind as she made goo-goo eyes with a blond Adonis at the end of the bar. Natalie knew she was seconds away from being dumped for the imitation Greek god, even before Megan turned to meet her gaze.

"Oh fuck it, just go," Natalie quipped as Megan's mouth opened.

"You're the best! I love you!" Meg squealed and kissed her cheek. "Have fun! See you later!"

"Humph." Sulking in her chair with a heavy sigh, Natalie's lips curled in disgust as Megan vanished into the crowd. Well, at least now she wouldn't have to worry about being caught when she bolted out the front door. *Damn them!* she thought. They practically dragged her here, and then deserted her. *Oh I will get them back*, she vowed. Finishing her drink and setting the glass on the marble-topped bar, she stood up to leave.

"Hello, Natalie. Leaving so soon?" a deep masculine voice purred close to her ear.

Natalie jumped at the intimate proximity of the stranger's body, but realized someone would have to be fairly close in order to be heard over the noise. Instantly recognizing the husky timbre of the voice, she spun around and bumped into a solid chest. The man standing in front of her grasped her arms to brace her unbalance. "Max," she gasped.

Her face turned bright red with embarrassment at being caught by her hunky co-worker in the BDSM club. Natalie tried to rein in her composure and silently willed her puckered nipples to recede. She didn't have any luck. The twin peaks were rock hard, standing at attention, begging for his touch.

Max Renfrew was the head of publications at the magazine where she worked and, since her first day, she'd had an enormous crush on him.

"Buy you a drink?" he asked, leaning close. His warm breath wafting across her cheek and ear made her shiver. Cocking his head playfully, his lips curled.

Although he exuded unchallenging confidence in his position as head of publications, he appeared rather shy in casual situations. On several occasions, Natalie had tried to engage Max in friendly conversation, but getting him to open up about anything other than work had been unsuccessful. Eventually, Natalie respected that Max was a private person wanting to keep his home life separate from his work life. Natalie understood, but she'd wanted to get to know him outside of the workplace. She knew nothing about him and neither did any of her co-workers.

Finally, conceding defeat where Max Renfrew was concerned, at least personally, she kept their encounters strictly work related. Besides, she really wanted someone a little more dominant to compliment her slightly submissive side. Natalie was very surprised to see him in the club, and hoped her expression didn't reveal her thoughts.

"I wandered in for a beer," he began looking over the mostly naked crowd. "I admit I've been curious about this place." He offered her a lopsided grin. "Please, don't leave me to drink alone."

Natalie swallowed the lump forming in her throat, and returned his smile. Suddenly, she was very nervous in his presence. She'd never realized before just how tall and broad he was. Physically, Max was exceptional. Although she'd only ever seen him clothed in fine tailored suits, and on the rare occasion a dress shirt after shedding his suit jacket, he appeared to take very good care of his body. Neatly coiffed dirty-blond, wavy hair hung just below his ears, and she dreamily imagined running her fingers through it. His eyes were deep, dark liquid chocolate and his gentle smile was infectious. Max wasn't drop dead gorgeous, but his striking features were beyond just handsome and revved Natalie's libido more often than not. On more than one occasion she'd made a mad dash to the ladies room to clean up. As she stood beside him, his nearness and the scent of his fresh, clean cologne overwhelmed her.

"Um, sure, Max... Okay," Natalie stammered.

"Excellent," he said and helped her back up onto the bar stool, seating himself beside her. He gave their order to the bartender Natalie hadn't noticed watching them. "Whatever the lady was drinking, and

I'll have a domestic draft, please." Max placed a twenty-dollar bill on the bar and turned his attention back to Natalie. When their drinks arrived, he told the bartender to keep the change.

Max was easy to talk to and equally willing to engage in dialogue. This was a nice change from the fellow at the office, and Natalie thought it encouraging. After a couple more beverages, Natalie glanced at her watch and realized they had talked away two and half hours, and not once did their conversation stray towards work. At the deep timbre of Max's voice, Natalie realized she'd been staring at him as her thoughts wandered.

"Would you excuse me for a minute," he said leaning toward her. "I'll be right back."

"Yes, of course. I'll wait here," she replied.

As Max disappeared into the crowd of undulating, sweating bodies, Natalie's mind began to wander again, this time with very naughty, unladylike thoughts. The sight of Max's dark eyes looking up at her from between her spread thighs, as his tongue laved her moist pussy, teased her mind.

A chill ran through her and she felt the warmth of a blush rise from her chest. A sexy hum slid past her lips. A vision of sucking his thick, silky cock down her throat, made her nipples taut and the tiny bundle of nerves between her legs begin to throb. She took a deep breath, then a mouthful of her drink, and fanned herself with her hand, blinking several times trying to clear the hedonistic images from her thoughts.

No luck.

Her mind continued to spin fantasies of her sexy boss.

In her head, she was on her back with her legs wrapped around Max's waist as he pounded himself into her over and over, her breasts rubbing erotically against his perfect, sculpted chest making her nipples tender and achy. As her mind's eye watched them fuck each other silly, Natalie was positive she could actually smell their sex and sweat.

Electricity tingled in the tips of her toes, teasing as it worked its way up the length of her spine. At the quickening of her pulse Natalie's top lip quivered, becoming damp with perspiration. The juncture between her thighs soaked her panties and her nipples ached as they distended into painful peaks. The heaving of her bosom increased as she struggled to draw air into her oxygen starved lungs.

As her arousal pushed her over the erotic edge into sated bliss, a shudder coursed through her body. Natalie gripped the bar bracing herself and closing her eyes, attempted to catch her breath. *Damn, my panties are drenched*! Her clit pulsed. She'd fucking come just *thinking* about having sex with Max!

The bartender appeared and set a bottle of water in front of her smiling knowingly. "This place can sometimes do that to a person." He offered an amused wink before wandering away.

Her mind started to spin. *What the hell is wrong with me*?

"I've got to get out of here," she whispered to herself. "I need some air."

* * * *

From the other end of the bar he observed her, unnoticed. Blending in with the other patrons no one would pay him any mind. After all, he was a just another client here to indulge in his fetish, and the object of that indulgence sat no more than thirty feet away.

Within the crush of near nude bodies, the distinctive odors of sweat and alcohol, blended with impending sexual satisfaction, surrounded him. The fragrance of her subtle perfume wafted across the room to taunt him. Her scent was infused in his mind, he'd recognize it anywhere.

He watched her tremble and knew the cause. Sparkling in the depths of her silver-blue eyes, he'd seen the repressed passion she refused to allow herself to experience. Through the intensity of his gaze, he'd helped to pull those animalistic thoughts to the forefront of her subconscious, preparing her for what was to come. Even at this distance, as her body trembled, he caught the scent of her arousal and creamy release.

He couldn't believe she had come.

With fierce determination, he ached to taste her.

His cock was steel hard, pressing painfully against the leather pants restraining it.

He could not believe his good fortune when she had finally walked through the doors of his club.

She was about to become his, and he would have her *begging* for no one else, but him.

* * * *

As she stood and turned to head for the exit for some fresh air, Natalie spotted a hooded man standing at the end of the bar, watching her. The black leather covering hid all but his eyes, a sliver of nose and mouth from her view. Eyes, dark brown, almost black stared back at her. The flaring of his nostrils kept time with the expansion of his broad, hairless chest as he drew breath. Full lips were pressed in a thin line, yet a smug grin curled the right side. Swallowing her nervousness, a heated chill coursed through her at his intense scrutiny. *Where the hell is Max*, she thought scanning the crowd.

The thought of Troy Simon's declaration opening night, fed her need to flee. She had to get the hell out of there. With wide eyes, Natalie groaned as the hooded man rose and stalked toward her.

She was being hunted.

Natalie guessed what was on his mind, and she was not about to be a party to it.

Straining her neck in a desperate search for an exit sign, she was jostled amongst the dancing crowd. She found none. Very quickly, she became disoriented, bumping around the gyrating, leather-clad mob, and the location of the front door was lost to her. The room began to tip as she frantically searched for an escape route.

Natalie felt his presence behind her, before the heat of his hands encircled her upper arms. As she struggled for breath, she felt her heart cease to beat. Her body broke out in a cold sweat and she licked her lips trying to get her salivary glands working once again.

No fucking luck.

"You...are mine," his deep, seductive voice reverberated through her trembling body.

"I...I...was...just...leaving," she mewled hoarsely.

"Before our fun begins?" The sensual voice teased her left ear.

Natalie froze unable move. Confident hands gripped her arms firmly.

"Breathe," he whispered against her cheek.

At the command, she shuddered and inhaled.

A masculine scent engulfed her, making her think of power, danger... dominance. The heat emanating from his body was electric and sparked Natalie's arousal. Her body responded to his intimidating presence, feeling a fire ignite in her lower belly. Every fine hair on her body stood on end, anticipating his next move.

She did not have long to wait.

"Come with me," he ordered, moving her through the crowd.

Her brain screamed '*NO*,' but her feet complied.

Stupid fucking body, she growled silently, as he directed her from behind. She felt the heat of his solid erection through his leather pants as it rubbed erotically against her suede-clad backside.

The crowd seemed to part like the Red Sea as Natalie and the hooded, hulking stranger made their way through. No one met her pleading glance as the masked man ushered her up a circular staircase.

Natalie's heart thumped an erratic tattoo against her rib cage. In a meek attempt to struggle, she was unable to free herself from the man's firm grasp. A giggle threatened to burst free from her lips at the feeble attempt, and her arousal soared higher. When they reached the top, two men clad in a similar fashion as the man behind her, stood on either side of the staircase. The knowing grins they flashed matched the amusement in their eyes, and Natalie's breath grew ragged as she and her escort continued down a darkened corridor.

This is wrong, she pleaded with her aroused body to stop and fight the stranger holding her. She felt his chest tight against her back as he held her to him. He steered her from behind to another set of stairs at the end of the long, dark hallway. Up they climbed to a third level and walked through a doorway at the top. They stopped momentarily and Natalie heard a latch click as the stranger locked the door behind them. He pushed her stiff body into a dark room, which he maneuvered them through, effortlessly. A second latch clicked before her surroundings illuminated, dimly. Natalie blinked several time adjusting to the sudden light.

"Strip," he ordered.

Natalie spun around. Looking up at her hooded escort, she glared angrily at him. "I will not," she spat out.

Without warning, his arm jerked.

Whoosh...SNAP

Natalie jumped at the sound splitting the air and caught sight of the handle of a whip in her captor's hand. A large fist closed tight around a braided end. The six-foot leather length which started at the handle a half-inch wide, tapered to a point that now lay on the polished hardwood floor, beside her left shoe. *Where did that come from?* she wondered, gnawing at her bottom lip. The atmosphere inside the room was scintillating. Natalie found herself quivering with excitement and a hint of fear. *Would he actually strike me with the whip?*

"Strip," he commanded in a harsh tone. With his lips drawn tight, his dark eyes dared her to refuse.

Natalie stood stunned, continuing to stare at the length of the whip in his hand.

Oh shit! How in the hell am I going to get out of this?

"Strip!"

Whoosh...SNAP

"*Eek!*" Natalie squealed and tugged her sleeveless knit top over her head. Reaching behind she unzipped her mini and pushed it over her hips to the floor and kicked it away. Her nipples pressed painfully against the red lacy demi bra she wore And dammit if her juices weren't flooding her pussy, dampening her panties. *Un-fucking-believable,* she chastised her betraying body, *this is just not right.*

"You are enjoying this," he stated with a smug grin.

"I am not!" Natalie retorted.

He reached up and pinched her nipple through her bra, hard. "Your body is."

[26]

Natalie swatted his hand away. "How dare you take liberties..."

He chuckled low, smiling at her irritation.

She scowled at him.

He reached again and with two fingers, effortlessly flicked the front closure of her bra, spilling its ample contents.

Natalie shrieked and made a feeble attempt to cover herself.

With lightening speed, large hands grabbed her wrists, raising her arms above her head, high enough to rock her balance, and he lowered his mouth to hers. His tongue possessively swept inside, tasting her, exploring her. Natalie's tongue joined the rest of her body in betrayal and began eagerly mating with his. The taste of him was hypnotic and delicious. Sucking the very breath from her lungs, she felt him probe even deeper.

* * * *

As her lips parted to protest, he took the invitation to invade the moist, warm cavern. Only when he felt her fervor match his own, did he pull away. Her eager response as she welcomed his kiss excited him. On her sweet tongue, the unmistakable growing need as she kissed him back left him a little light-headed.

Quickly, he reined in his escalating arousal. He couldn't afford to allow her to get the upper hand, he was the Dom after all. It had been a dream of his for so very long, to make her submit to him. Lowering her arms, he slid the straps of her bra down and off her body. Eyes, vague and dreamy, looked up at him, revealing how much she seemed to enjoy the aftermath of his oral exploration.

Ah, but he was only just beginning. Inside his pants, his cock ached. He needed to release himself before he burst... but not quite yet.

First, she must come for him.

This was his fantasy and he intended to live it to the fullest. Hell, he might not get a repeat performance. Restraining her hands behind her back with his left hand, he brought up his right to cup the soft mound of her left breast. Again, he lowered his lips to hers to stifle her gasp of protest.

Refusal would not be allowed.

Massaging the heavy globe in his palm, his fingers tugged at the throbbing, peaked nipple. Tilting her back, he felt the damp, heat of her pussy press against his straining cock. He continued to tug at her nipple until she was near sobbing, trembling from his touch. When he released her mouth, she struggled to suck air into her oxygen-starved lungs.

As his lips and tongue burned a wet trail down her throat, his wandering hand slid into the front of her panties and thick fingers began exploring what lay hidden beneath the lacy fabric. A single, thick digit pushed inside her and she whimpered. The scent of her arousal flooded his nostrils. He inhaled deeply.

"You're already so wet for me," he said pushing the length of his finger deeper, until his palm rested against her now throbbing clit. His finger and palm worked together building the heat inside her until she was choking on sobs with every breath.

Adding another finger into her tight heat, he stroked a rhythm that stole her breath. Tipping her over further, he latched onto a nipple, suckling it with the same zeal as his thrusting fingers.

Natalie's self-control shattered. Her body belonged to him. He commanded it, no longer was she free thinking. Her heart raced, her body alight, humming from an erotic charge as he coaxed her higher. A stitch in her lower back began screaming. The tips of her finger tingled, and there was a sting in her shoulders from being restrained in an awkward position for so long. No longer could she feel her toes. Under persuasive, demanding fingers, her mind became numb to her surroundings. At the moment, nothing else mattered except the animalistic carnality this hooded stranger was wringing from her very, eager body.

Try as she might, she couldn't stop herself from giving in to his ministration. Expert fingers played her as though she was made only for him, his tongue and lips were magic as they devoured her. She wanted them all over her, kissing, sucking, licking... biting.

Oh God how she wanted him to bite her. The thought of his teeth nipping her tender flesh made her tremble.

He felt her desperate need as if it were his own. Pulling her upright, he released the hands he'd restrained. The fingers of his right hand thrust into her warm pussy, while his left ventured in search of the tight pucker of her ass. As his finger dipped between her buttocks, he found the crack slick from the juices he'd helped create. He rolled his finger in the wetness before plunging the long, thick digit inside her tight asshole. When he entered the snug, velvety heat, Natalie flung her arms around his neck, clinging to him. His thrusting fingers, impaling her, barely held her upright.

Head thrown back, he watched the play of emotions cross her face as the violent climax rocked through her. The flesh surrounding his fingers convulsed, pulsing with each rippling wave that assaulted her. Forcing her to climb even higher, he watched her tremble as she rode his pleasuring hands and fingers.

He owned her. She belonged to him. The sound of her cry echoed around and through him.

"Ahh!" Her eyes rolled back in her head as another explosive orgasm coursed through her, flexing against his digits.

Around his probing fingers her slick heat tightened once again, and the sound of her cries was music to his ears. Suddenly, her grip around his neck weakened and he withdrew his drenched fingers from her quivering body. Reveling in the sated look he found in her half closed eyes, her soft flesh glistened, her cheeks, flushed.

"You're so beautiful," he whispered hoarsely. His cock throbbed near to bursting, as he held her.

He had only a split second to react as Natalie fell limp into his arms.

He'd finger fucked her to passing out. Extremely pleased with himself, a smug grin crossed his face.

And he was so very far from finished.

CHAPTER 2

Natalie awoke disoriented her muscles achy, head bent forward, eyes closed.

The warmth and electricity of a body pressed against her back. Hot breath caressed her left ear and neck as a deep sultry voice brought her senses to attention.

"Welcome back." He purred.

As she regained some semblance of consciousness, she felt her body splayed, upright, in an 'X' formation. The heat of two large, strong hands rested on her hips, gripping her. Fingers and thumbs kneaded her soft flesh. A shudder raced through her body at the seductive tone and she felt her nipples pucker. Her eyes shot open. With her head still forward, in the dimly lit room she had a clear view of the excited peaks of her naked breasts. Glancing a little lower, confusion laced with panic ripped through her. Her torso was now covered in a tight black leather corset, coming to a stop just under her breasts, giving the illusion of an offering.

Natalie snapped her head up abruptly, smacking against a solid mass behind her. With a *thunk*, she saw stars and winced, startled at the sudden stop. "Oh God," Natalie gasped in horror at the sight before her. Her eyes grew wide and she was suddenly chilled to the bone.

She stared at her own reflection.

Her curly strawberry-blond hair hung loose to cascade over her shoulders. Clothed only in the corset, she was strapped to a metal pillory, with her head left free. Leather restraints bound her arms on either side above her head, her ankles shackled wide apart at the base. Two thin straps attached to the corset ran between her legs, pulling the plump outer lips of her sex open, exposing the swollen, wet bud inside. Natalie could see her clit glisten in the dim light, and her thighs were slick and shiny.

Staring back at herself in the mirror, Natalie watched his hand reach up to cup her right breast and fingers squeezed her nipple, rolling it roughly between thumb and forefinger. Without moving, her eyes shifted to the reflection of the hooded masculine figure standing behind her. The soft gasp that escaped her brought a smile to his full lips. Eyes, heavy with desire looked back at her in the mirror, and her heart skipped a beat. Moisture flooded her sex and the ache in her breasts grew painful. A musky spice assaulted her senses, creating a pleasurable throb in the bundle of nerves between her legs. The tips of her fingers tingled and she wanted to reach out and touch him. Firm biceps flexed as he stroked her heating flesh. The man stood a head taller than the unrecognizable woman on the pillory, and she felt dwarfed and uncomfortable, bound and exposed before him.

"You came so hard for me you passed out." Full lips parted and a husky voice caressed over her. "You were only out a few minutes though. Jesus, you're so beautiful when you come." While his right hand continued to torment her right nipple, his left ventured across and down her abdomen cupping her exposed cunt.

"Oh my God," Natalie groaned as a long, thick finger pushed up inside her.

The finger withdrew and then stroked her inner thigh.

"Look at your come slicked thighs... The only thing that would look sexier would be my come dripping out of your sweet pussy, running down those smooth legs, along with yours. Mmm, very soon."

He brought his finger up to his mouth and licked it clean. "You taste so good. I'm going to enjoy eating your pussy and making you come all over my tongue."

Natalie couldn't speak as she stared at the reflection of the masked man behind her, unable to remember how she ended up in this situation. She'd been out with...

His deep voice, along with the movement of his hands, brought her attention back to him. "We've only just begun. I'm not done playing with you yet. You're going to come again for me," he promised.

The smooth fingertips on her breast pinched tighter and a finger was pushed into her body again. A steady rhythm had Natalie whimpering as she rode his hand. Two more fingers slide inside her heat while his thumb assaulted her swollen clit in firm, tight circles.

Natalie's eyes were half closed as the stranger behind her finger-fucked her, making her body soar. What the hell had lead to her being strapped next to naked to a pillory for the sexual enjoyment of a hooded hulking stranger? *Jesus.* She moaned aloud, the ability to think straight gone from her grasp. Thick fingers moved inside her with exquisite expertise. Far from a virgin, in her limited experience, Natalie had never been a part of anything like this.

She glimpsed into the mirror before her and met the piercing gaze of the hooded man, slicing into her soul. Dark eyes were riveted on the passionate expression etched on her face, as his hands worked their magic urging her toward release. With her head resting against the strong right shoulder behind her, his long wet tongue licked across her bare shoulder up the length of her neck to circle the curve of her ear. A shiver of arousal from the heat of his wet caress and the sight of his fingers disappearing inside the slick folds of her pussy, coursed up the length of her spine. The tugging on her nipple increased...to the point of hurting.

Her tormentor's breath was as ragged as her own. The muscles in Natalie's cunt gripped thrusting fingers as he increased his intimate stroking. His right hand wrapped around, cupping her left breast as he held her tight to his chest. "Come for me, Natalie," he commanded hoarsely. "Come now."

"*Oh fuck,*" she groaned as a powerful orgasm ripped through her.

Her body no longer belonged to her. It was completely under his control. As she pulsed with release, she was nothing more than putty in his masterful hands. Her knees gave out from under her, forcing his fingers even deeper inside. The restraints binding her wrists held her up, but dug into her flesh. The arm wrapped around her waist lifted her back to standing, while his fingers continued driving her to another explosive climax. This time after her body shuddered, he pulled his slick fingers from her body, coated in her cream and brought them to his mouth for a taste. As he savored her essence on his tongue, a groan of satisfaction filled her ears.

Somewhere off in the distance, Natalie heard the rattle of buckles and had little control over her arms as the bindings were tugged free. The tips of her fingers tingled as blood once again flowed to them. Through the fog clouding her brain, Natalie felt herself being lowered to the floor. Her breath was harsh, and her body trembled with aftershocks of two rocking orgasms. As she lay slumped he came around and stood before her.

With effort, she glanced up at the enormous hooded man. Christ he was huge, towering over her vulnerable quivering body. A leather harness with straps crisscrossing over a broad, hairless chest adorned his masculine perfection. Dark chocolate nipples were tight peaks against tanned skin. Natalie's mouth watered and she ached to taste his flesh.

What the hell is happening to me? This is so wrong, she tried to tell herself.

Black leather strips wrapped around well defined biceps. Her eyes wandered lower and the straps of the harness around his torso, connected to straps wrapping the tops of his powerful thighs, drawing her attention to the dangerous looking beast dangling between. His pubic hair was groomed close to his body, leaving just a dark dusting of color.

Unabashed, he stood before her.

The slit at the end of his semi-erect cock was moist with pre-cum as it grew harder under her watchful eye. Natalie couldn't take her eyes off it. It was a monster and it just grew harder and longer.

"Suck me," he commanded.

Her eyes grew wide as they met his heated gaze. "But...I..."

His right hand raised and dropped like a flash and a crack split the air.

Whoosh...SNAP

"Oh!" Natalie gasped shielding herself, expecting to feel the bite of the leather whip.

It didn't come. She looked at him expectantly.

"Wrap those beautiful lips around my cock and suck me." His stern voice made her tremble at his feet. "If you don't pleasure me well, I will punish you."

Natalie jumped at the tone of his voice, scrambling to her feet and squatted before him, her ankles still bound. *What the hell have those two got me into?* she thought as she looked up at the hooded man and tried to gather moisture into her dry mouth. Flicking her tongue out, she ran it over her lips to wet them. She wrapped her fingers around the solid nine inches of cock dancing in front of her face and stroked his length a couple of times. Her slender digits were nowhere near close to touching as they wrapped around him. *Christ he was so thick.*

Leaning forward, Natalie parted her lips and flicked her tongue over the smooth head, dipping into the dripping slit at the end. Salty pre-cum teased her taste buds and she suddenly wanted more of him. The excitement arousing her startled her. Closing her lips around him, she drew his length to the back of her throat. As her tongue teased the underside of his cock, a groan from deep within his chest vibrated through her core. His moans and groans grew harsh and intense as she stroked and sucked.

Fingers tangled in her hair as he grabbed a fist full of her strawberry blond curls. "That's good...real good. Just like that," he groaned.

With her left hand, Natalie reached up cupping his tight sac and palmed his testicles. Chancing a firmer squeeze on his tender package, the grip in her hair tightened, to the point of near pain, and her pussy flooded with liquid heat at the exciting, foreign sensation.

Pain pleasurable? She thought.

"Oh God, woman," his raspy voice growled low, bucking his hips against her face.

Natalie knew she succeeded in pleasing him by his body's movements and guttural sounds. She found herself growing more and more turned on as the satisfied gasps and groans escaped the hooded stranger's lips. Despite the situation and the fact she had yet to learn his name, Natalie no longer found him threatening. He hadn't hurt her. He *had* tormented her with sexual pleasure. And there was something else she felt–something familiar about the hooded stranger...she just couldn't quite put her finger on it. From the fire licking within, her body began to burn. Oh how she desperately wanted to, needed to pleasure him well. Natalie wanted control over his body, just as he had over hers, and the thought of possessing that power, aroused her more.

Sucking him harder, deeper, her hands continued to palm his heavy sac. She worked on his shaft with such ferocity she'd started to drool around the thick cock in her mouth. Glancing up to gage the expression on his face, well, what she could see, her breath caught. His eyes were dark with desire, glassy and focused on her mouth. The smile curling his full lips on one side, reached his eyes.

"Fuck, look at you. You are sexier at this moment than I think I've ever seen you," he said huskily. "The sight of your luscious lips wrapped around my cock...uh Christ," he groaned.

As Natalie wiped the spit hanging from her bottom lip, she was struck with a very naughty idea. Could she be so brazen? She'd *never* done anything like that before. She had heard some men enjoyed it, but would this masked man? *Hell, what do I have to lose?*

Sliding her hand between his thighs, she squeezed the cheeks of his more than firm ass. Shit, the man was solid muscle every-fucking-where! The thrusting of his hips pushing his cock deeper into her eager mouth gave Natalie the answer for her internal query. Slipping a wet finger between the globes, she sought out the puckered rosette hidden within. Firmly caressing the surrounding area and rim, made him groan. With gentle pressure, Natalie pressed against the tight outer muscles until they opened, and her finger slipped inside.

Natalie heard his sharp intake of breath and felt a shudder course through him. Smiling around his cock, she continued to work her index finger inside. This being her first time fingering a man's ass, she wasn't entirely sure what to do. Continuing to feel her way around, Natalie finally found what she sought. Her fingertip grazed over the hard knot of what she suspected was his prostate.

"Oh fuck," was growled above as she stroked her fingertip over the sweet spot, making his cock jerk between her lips.

Ah, she'd struck gold! She pressed harder on the little button her finger had found.

"Ah fuck, woman!" was groaned just seconds before hot salty liquid spilled from his slit, shooting down the back of her throat.

Natalie sucked hungrily at the pulsing cock as her finger continued to stroke him inside. She swallowed and swallowed unsure if he'd ever empty. It didn't matter, he tasted divine and she didn't want to miss a single drop. She couldn't get enough of his taste, his scent, the feel of him beneath her fingers.

She slowed the wet strokes of her mouth and licked his slit clean before pulling back. As Natalie looked up releasing his balls and withdrawing her finger from his ass, she found him gripping either side of the pillory, white knuckled, his breath harsh, his body shaking gently. His eyes squeezed tightly shut.

After taking several moments to catch his breath, his eyes opened and he looked down at her. "Good girl," he said hoarsely through panted breath. Kneeling, he unfastened the shackles around her ankles, and she studied his covered face, trying to read his further intentions. His expression was back to blank. As the second clasp released, his eyes met hers.

Natalie swallowed the lump, lodged in her throat.

"Stand up and follow me," he ordered.

Natalie struggled to get to her feet. As she stood, she took in the surroundings of the room. She was in a dungeon, like she'd seen on one of those sex documentaries about fetishes. Oh hell, she remembered finally. She'd come to Le Club d'Esclavage with Dani and Megan, and now she was being used as a BDSM slave for some pervert.

Floor to ceiling mirrors adorned all four walls, and various uncomfortable looking apparatuses decorated the open space. Whips and paddles hung on racks, and benches shelved lubes and dildos and vibrators in a variety of colors, shapes and sizes.

The straps between her legs were annoying the hell out of her and treading dangerously close to disappearing between the cheeks of her ass. She reached to adjust the offending material.

"Don't touch," he warned without turning.

"But it's going up my ass," she argued sharply. "And listen, I'm tired of playing this game. Where's the door, I'm getting the hell out of here." Natalie padded barefoot across the room and stopped less than a foot before him. She raised her hand to poke a finger into his muscled chest and opened her mouth to chew him out.

Full lips crashed against hers, kissing her with a fierceness that took her breath away and weakened her knees. His hands grabbed hers, twisting them behind her back as he assaulted her mouth with an exploring tongue. Natalie grew dizzy with the euphoric sensations thrumming through her body. Her nipples grew hard, pebble-like, and her pussy flooded with her essence. Spinning her around with her arms raised above her head, he lowered her into a sling-type apparatus. When her ass hit the seat, she jerked up against him.

"Ah, you've finally felt the plug," he uttered smoothly.

"Plug? What plug?" She said with irritation. "What the hell did you do to me?"

"I inserted a butt plug in that tight little asshole of yours," his voice was sultry as he fastened her ankles once again. "The straps are holding the plug in place." He rose and disappeared behind her.

"You what?" she growled her irritation. "Why the hell would you do that?" *And why the hell hadn't I noticed the fucking thing before now?* No, it didn't hurt, and it wasn't terribly uncomfortable... but she now knew the damn thing was there.

Damned, if it didn't feel...kind of good.

A light hum filled the room and the apparatus where she sat, began to elevate.

* * * *

The heated look on her face made his cock twitch against his thigh. She was feisty, irate, and sexy as hell. And tonight, she was all his.

"I want you hot, ready and open for me when I fuck your ass, my little slave."

"Slave? I'm not your fucking slave, pal, now let me down from here," she growled, squirming against the restraints.

"Talk like that will get you paddled, slave. *You* are my sex slave for as long as I choose to keep you here," he whispered with confidence against her ear. "And I'm having a *ton* of fun right now." The trembling of her body, made his balls ache. He enjoyed watching her body react as he informed her of her fate. "That's the rules of the club. You were aware of the rules before you entered, weren't you!" He asked with a deep chuckle, knowing damn well she was since her magazine had covered their opening, thoroughly. He also knew she'd read every article.

Natalie went still in the sling.

The bobbing of her throat indicated the effort it took for her to swallow. "Wha...what rules?" She croaked, meeting his gaze in the mirror.

He stood behind her studying her, and loved what he saw. Before him she sat, her luscious, ample tits heaved with her breath, just for his enjoyment, nipples hard and begging, her thighs spread wide, and her slick, wet pussy open to his hungry gaze. She was bound, helpless, with a pleading look in her beautiful silvery blue eyes as she watched him closely. God he'd dreamed of having her just like this, and now here she was, available for his every sexual whim.

"You're keeping me here against my will," she pleaded with a quivering lower lip.

With a smug smile, he shook his head. "I'm not holding you against your will, you want this."

"What! Where in the hell did you get the idea I wanted you to tie me up and *use* me?"

"You walked through the door of the club willingly. You were not dragged in here kicking and screaming, were you? One very important rule of Le Club d'Esclavage, which is very public and very clear, is you only enter the club if you want to experience the lifestyle. There are many different levels of the BDSM lifestyle, but first timers or visitors here, are treated to a 'light' experience during their virgin visit." He watched her shudder again and relished the sound of the air leaving her lungs in a flustered rush. He studied her closely as she processed his words.

"They knew", she grumbled low. "I'll kill them," she muttered still studying him.

Her comment made him smirk. "Who?" He asked already knowing the answer. He'd watched their arrival from his apartment on the top floor.

"My soon to be *ex*-friends," she growled through gritted teeth.

He had to get Natalie back to that passionate state where he'd taken her before. He loved the look of exquisite pleasure suffusing her beautiful features as she came at his hand. The way she squeezed her eyes closed, her cute little nose wrinkled up, and the way she bit her lower lip. Just thinking about it made his cock swell with need again. He had to sink himself into her hot channel soon before he went fucking crazy. Sliding his hands down her back he cupped her bare buttocks, massaging their warmth. The sling left her ass and pussy open for his taking. He slipped a finger along the crack of her ass and wiggled the plug.

"Huhhh!" Natalie sucked in air.

He chuckled against her cheek before placing a light kiss there. "Do you like that?"

"It feels...different...but, sort of...good," she answered, and the heated desire in her eyes told him she spoke the truth.

"Well then," he wiggled the plug again, "It's time to continue playing my little slave." He walked over to a set of shelves to grab some supplies. After gathering what he needed, he walked around and knelt facing her.

"What are you going to do to me?" Natalie asked, a bit breathless.

"Whatever I want," he admitted with confidence. He reached up and stroked the back of his fingers across her blushing cheek.

The path his fingers took burned a trail down the hollow of her throat and over the swell of her right breast to her nipple. Blunt fingertips pulled at the puckered bud until Natalie whimpered at the pleasure burn he created. His fingers moved to her neglected nipple where he tugged and pulled until she gasped, thrusting her chest forward. The harsh panting she could not control.

Through her half closed eyes, she saw his left hand rise holding something, metal-like. In his fingers the hooded man held two small clamps connected by a chain. Wide-eyed she watched him fasten one of the metal, alligator-type clips to her distended right nipple. Natalie gasped out loud as it tightened on the aching peak. She groaned as the second was clipped onto her left nipple.

"Oh my," she panted and her face heated.

"Does that feel good?"

"Yes," she moaned.

"Yes what?"

"Yes it feels good," Natalie wriggled in the sling trying to make some contact with the butt plug in her backside.

"The correct response is, yes, 'Master'," he said.

Her eyes popped open. "You're fucking joking, right?"

"Say, yes, Master," his expression harsh, voice firm.

Natalie shook her head. *No way am I calling him 'master'. Who the fuck does this guy think he is?*

The sharp tug on the chain linking the nipple clamps made her cry out. A sting zinging through the tips of her breasts shot straight to the juncture between her thighs. She found the splinter of pain arousing, and the warm tingle of another orgasm began to build inside her. In anticipation, Natalie grew anxious wondering where he would lead her next.

"*Oh...yes*, Master...yes, Master," she croaked.

"Good girl," he praised and brushed his thumbs over the tender peaks of her breasts.

His gaze travelled to the slickness between her legs, he reached out, and dragged his fingertip along her opening. Natalie's own eyes watched as his finger disappeared inside her. When he withdrew from her heat, his finger glistened with her wetness. As he pushed into her again, she tightened her muscles against his intrusion.

"Mmmm that's very nice, my slave. I want your cunt to grip my cock just like this when I shove it into this tight little hole of yours."

Natalie shivered at his words and groaned.

Several strokes he pumped his thick finger into her before finally withdrawing. Turning his head, he reached for something beside him and brought a slender, smooth pink vibrator into view.

"Oooh," she sighed as he slipped it between his lips and rolled his tongue over its length, moistening it, and then aligned it with the mouth of her sex.

Dipping his head, eyes fixed on hers, he drew his tongue up the length of her wet slit, flicking the tip across her clit, which now throbbed with need. He pulled back and pushed the tip of the vibrator into her body.

"No," Natalie whimpered unconvincingly.

The masked man continued to push, until eight inches of the toy had vanished in her depths. With a twist of the shiny pink toy, he pulled it out of her pussy. She wiggled trying to impale herself on the device as he slowly reinserted it inside her. He continued his painfully slow torture as she writhed in the sling restraining her. Suddenly the heat of his mouth closed around her clit as he thrust the solid plastic toy in and out of her.

The wet slurp of her pussy sucking at the phallus brought a smile to his lips. *Christ she is so wet and so hot, all by my hands.* Her eyes, as she looked at him, were heavy with desire, need, begging for the culmination he alone could bring her.

He sucked hungrily at her swollen clit, dipping his tongue inside her pussy alongside the vibrator. Natalie's body jerked when he turned the dial at the end, bringing the toy to life. Again he tugged at the chain linking the clamps clipped on her nipples as he worked the vibrating toy in and out of her pussy.

She panted, struggling for movement in the sling. "Please, Master..." she moaned.

He smiled as she remembered to use his title.

"Please what, my beautiful slave?" He sucked her swollen clit harder.

"Oh God, Master..." She wiggled against his feasting mouth, driving the toy deeper. "Please, Master, please fuck me," Natalie begged. "I want to feel you inside me...only you..."

His aching cock throbbed and he damn near shot his load all over the floor. *Jesus, she is fucking beautiful spread out before me like this.* A light sheen of perspiration glistened on her soft skin and her pussy dripped her arousal. He leaned over and licked a rivulet of salty sweat trickling between her heaving breasts. Her lips quivered as she gasped sobs of pleasure, her wrists an angry red, as she pulled against the restraints in a futile effort to touch him.

Unable to deny either of them any longer, he rose up on his knees pulling the toy from Natalie's body, aligned his weeping cock with the mouth of her tight passage, and with one hard, deliberate thrust, impaled her with his shaft.

"Oh God, Ma..." Somehow through the delirium, Natalie stopped herself from calling out Max's name, as she felt the hooded man embed his heavy, thick shaft to the hilt within her willing body.

During her entire time within the walls of the dungeon, she'd been thinking of Max. Wishing it was him dominating her, having his way with her, using her, making her beg with unquenched lust. She didn't know what the outcome of the current situation would be, but figured she might as well have a good time while she was here. And only caught in the crosshairs of a firing squad, would she admit to having the time of her life.

Natalie's groans of satisfaction drove him to pound even harder into her. Oh how he lost his very being within the heat of her body. She pulsed around him, milking his shaft with every withdrawal. As he slammed himself into her, he came to the startling realization she was his perfect match. Sexually, absolutely, but what he felt went deeper than that. She had no idea that she completed him as a man.

"Oh, Master," Natalie moaned, "I'm going to come for you,

Master... just for you." She tossed her head from side to side. "Please, Master, come with me. Please."

Her simple, pleading request was his undoing. He felt her muscles convulse around his impaling shaft as her body gave in to him yet again, his own climax taking him by surprise shooting his release inside her with a force he'd never felt before. "Oh, Natalie...Natalie..."

"Yes, Master...*yes*," she cried as her orgasm rocked her.

Spent, he collapsed against her bosom causing the sling to sway from their combined weight. Several moments passed before either one could speak.

He recovered first.

"Jesus, Natalie," he panted against her neck. "Do you have any idea what you do to me?"

Several moments passed, their labored breath, the only sound.

"Untie me," she softly murmured, "I want to touch you."

With effort, he reached one hand up to release the Velcro straps restraining his slave, grasping one hand, pulled it to his mouth to place a kiss on her palm. He refused to remove his lips from her flesh.

Natalie slid her free hand along the smooth leather hood still shielding his face from her, and then over his sweat-slicked skin. She stroked his back and shoulders with the gentle caress of a lover.

It was too much for him to hope for.

His still hard cock jerked inside her once again. A low growl sounded deep in his throat as he withdrew his shaft from her. Natalie whimpered at the emptiness in her pussy. Although she touched him, she ached to have him inside her body again. She enjoyed a euphoric contentment she'd never experienced in her life. Never had she been this sated! And all at the hands of a complete stranger, no less! Releasing her ankles, he stood and grabbed her hand, roughly pulling her over to a waist high bench, forcing her to lay her upper body across its padded surface, and gripped her hips in a tight, bruising hold.

"I have to fuck that beautiful ass of yours now," he said with raspy breaths as his hand slid around to the tops of her thighs, to release the straps holding her plump labia open.

Natalie sighed as the straps gave, combined with the feel of his hands stroking the cheeks of her ass. She felt his fingers in her crack and the movement of the plug. Gripping the flared base, he slowly eased it out of her. Natalie hissed as the widest part stretched her muscles a bit more on its exit. Cool lube smeared over her puckered opening and a thick finger pushed some inside her hole.

"I need you this way, Natalie, I really do," his voice gentle, soft and somewhat pleading. "May I?" he asked barely above a whisper.

Natalie shuddered.

With those two little words, he'd handed control over to her. *Was this a trick? Is his allowing me a say in how we continue, intentional?* Until now, the masked man had done what he wanted, when he wanted, she'd had no say. However, she had been willing and eagerly allowed him to do so. Without knowing, she had submitted to his seductive persuasion and loved every minute of it!

She smiled as the realization of what she felt, smacked her right upside the head. "My body is yours, Master...I am yours," she purred over her shoulder. Wiggling her backside, she added, "Yes, please...fuck my ass, Master."

Shaky fingers spread her buttocks wide and the smooth head of his cock pressed against the tight ring of muscles, slowly breeching her opening. Natalie sucked in a breath.

His entrance stilled. "Do you want me to stop?" He asked with concern.

Natalie panted, her body quivering. "Not if you know what's good for you."

She heard his sharp intake of breath and felt his body tremble as he continued to feed all nine fucking inches of thick, solid cock into her welcoming ass.

Once inside, he refrained from movement allowing her muscles to adjust and relax around his intrusion before sliding his thick length back out. Natalie hissed as the fat head of his shaft stretched her opening slightly before he pushed himself back into her velvet heat.

In his thoughts, he'd imagined she would feel good, but he had no idea just how fucking incredible her body would feel. He was going to explode in record time, and he desperately wanted to prolong this pleasure for both of them.

"Does my cock feel good in your ass, Natalie?"

"Oh God yes...yes, Master, your cock feels so good. Please, fuck me. I want you...I need you..." her voice pleaded with desperation.

He was beyond control. It took several strokes in the velvety heat of Natalie's ass and he was pumping himself into her. The tight canal pulsed around his shaft as he stilled, emptying himself into her. Exhausted, he collapsed on her back, her heartbeat kept time with his. Their bodies both slick with sweat. As he withdrew his softening cock from her ass, his release gushed from her body, dripping down the back of her thighs.

"I've never..." Natalie moaned harshly. "I've never felt as good as I do at this very minute." She chuckled. "I've never done anything like this before. I'm embarrassed that I don't even know your name."

He stiffened against her and silent moments passed before he lifted his weight off her. "That's part of the fantasy," he said gruffly, pulling away from her.

If she were to know who he was now, it would ruin everything.

Natalie stood slowly and turned around to face him. Studying her mysterious masked lover, a slight smile turned up one side of her mouth. Physically he was exquisite. His broad chest heaved as he attempted to get his breathing under control. Heavy perspiration glistened all over his muscular body. She could smell his masculine scent coating her flushed skin.

With confidence, she threw him a challenging glare.

"Bullshit," Natalie spewed. "Now take off that fucking hood," she demanded placing her hands on her hips.

His raised brow showed his surprise at her boldness and his lips parted as if he were about to protest.

All right, so he wasn't a hardcore enthusiast interested in inflicting pain for pleasure, sure a little bit was okay, but not entirely his thing. He enjoyed bondage, the use of toys and wanted a willing submissive partner who would enjoy acting out their fantasies together.

How dare Natalie order him to remove his hood? He was the Dom, dammit! He didn't take orders!

"Bullshit?" he repeated through gritted teeth.

Natalie looked his magnificent, naked body up and down with purpose. She had to see the face of the man who had thoroughly pleasured her, repeatedly taking her body to heights she never knew she could reach.

"That's what I said, *Master*," she stressed his 'title' with exaggerated deference. "Now get that fucking hood off. I want to see the face of the man who has wrung more pleasure from my body, than I ever thought possible."

She approached him and reached for the zipper running up the back of the hood before he had a chance to lift his own hand. Slowly, Natalie drew the zipper from the base of his neck to the crown of his head. Gripped both sides of the opening, she pulled it forward and off his head.

"You!"

CHAPTER 3

Natalie's body froze, her breath lodged in her throat, as her eyes took in the handsome face staring back at her. Finally managing a weak gasp, she dropped the leather hood to the floor at her feet.

"Why?"

He stroked the back of a finger across Natalie's cheek.

She shivered.

"Do you have any idea how long I've wanted you?" he asked.

"I've wanted you too, Max," she admitted, and although he was looking right at her, he didn't hear her declaration.

"How long I've wanted to get you here? How I've ached to be with you? I never thought you'd ever come into my club."

"This is your club?" she asked surprised.

"Yeah, it's all mine," he shrugged. "Right now we're in my private quarters on the top floor. I live right here on site," he admitted to her. "I've thought of no one else but you since you started at the magazine four years ago, Natalie. That's four long fucking years. I pull my cock so often thinking of you, it gets damn sore. I couldn't believe my luck when I watched you walk through the front door tonight."

Natalie stood stunned. All this time Max had wanted her, just as much as she had wanted him. She thought she'd been giving off all the right signals, and yet... No way, she wasn't going to dwell on the past miscommunications. They were together, here, now, and that is all that mattered to her. And she was not about to let him get away now. Especially after everything they'd shared tonight. Max had no idea he completed her, as a woman. There was absolutely no doubt in her mind...she was his.

Despite being tied up, which she found hot, she *had* given herself to him freely. She did come into the club of her own free will. Natalie had thoroughly enjoyed her introduction into the BDSM scene, and was glad her first time had been with Max.

When they spoke in the bar earlier in the evening, Natalie had decided she was going to seduce Max Renfrew, making him hers, if it was the last thing she ever did. Now she had been with him, however, he had done the seducing. "Did you slip something in my drink to get me up here with you?" she asked.

"No, I'd never drug you, Natalie, or anyone else, that's just not right," he replied and looked down at his feet.

Natalie's heart soared and her pussy grew wet! Dammit, she was ready for him again! She thought it cute that Max had turned shy all of a sudden. Very different from the dominant man she'd spent the last few hours with. She found his sudden 'submissiveness' a huge turn on, because she knew *exactly* what he could turn into!

"Well," she said and walked behind him toward a bench along one wall. She picked up a wooden paddle and tested its weight in her hand. As she turned toward him, she saw Max still had his back to her. He hadn't seen her pick up the paddle.

A sly smile crept across her face.

With his head hung low, his fingers twitched at his sides. He raised his head as she approached, her hand holding the paddle behind her back.

"I'm sorry, Natalie, you're probably really pissed with me right now."

Natalie gave a half nod, but didn't speak.

"I meant no harm, honestly. I wanted to be with you and I didn't know how to get you to notice me outside of work. Christ, Natalie, you make the office 'Max' really nervous."

She made him nervous? She nearly laughed out loud at his revelation. Shit, whenever Max Renfrew was around, she couldn't string a single sentence together. He unknowingly left her tongue tied and sexually frustrated. He had no idea how many nights she fucked herself with her vibrator, wishing it were his cock inside her. Maybe she'd share that little confession with him, later, because right now she had other things on her dirty little mind. "Well, Max, you've got my attention now," she purred.

Max still hadn't turned his body, so his firm left ass cheek was right there for her taking.

Begging her!

Natalie licked her lips as she met his gaze in the mirror. His dark brown eyes focused on the wet tip of her pink tongue as it darted out and over her lips.

"Now, slave, haul your ass to the pillory," she ordered him.

His head snapped to face her just as she swung the wooden paddle.

He didn't even see it coming.

WHACK

The sound of the paddle connecting with Max's firm ass cheek split the silence hanging between them.

Natalie shivered excitedly.

Max's eyes grew wide with surprise. The heat flickering in them matched hers.

* * * *

No way, Max thought. *Is she serious?* "Natalie?"

WHACK

Wielding the paddle a second time she connected with his twin ass cheek.

"I believe the title you're looking for, slave, is...'Mistress,'" she said, palming the paddle.

Max hesitated as he studied her, unsure he'd heard correctly, and when her lips curled up and her beautiful blue eyes flared with desire, he ran to the pillory. Bending to fasten the restraints around his own ankles, eagerly he replied, "Yes, my Mistress."

A Toy

For Two

CHAPTER 1

Earlier, Megan's best friend Dani had called to say she had the weekend off—the first in six weeks. The two of them planned to make tonight an event their other best friend Natalie would not soon forget.

At Dani's suggestion, they were taking Natalie to the hottest night club in the city to celebrate fun, friends, and freedom from the workplace. Le Club d'Esclavage had opened the year earlier, and its popularity grew every evening. By all reports, the BDSM club had been a bigger success than anyone first thought. Three months after opening night, management had already been forced to use guest list, and take reservations for the private playrooms on the second floor. If a customer didn't have an 'in', they could expect to spend hours in line waiting their turn to get inside.

Piled into a yellow taxi, the trio were on their way. Natalie had no idea what they had planned for her, and by the stoic expression of disinterest on her face, didn't particularly care. Megan knew Natalie had been pulling 24/7 days with a new client at the magazine where she worked, and would've been happier than a pig in shit to spend the evening alone catching up on her rest. Megan, however, was 'good time central', so with gentle but persistent encouragement from Dani, they'd talked Natalie into a girls' night out on the town.

Natalie was the sensible, level headed member of their trio. She'd had to study hard for good grades, worked several part-time jobs to put herself through school, and now dedicated every spare moment to her career.

Dani was the adorable, stereotypical blonde, which would be far more fitting if she weren't a brunette. She was fun loving, naïve and innocent to a fault. Her family didn't have the money to further her education after high school, so Dani worked the day shift at her parent's local coffee diner. She loved her job, and the customers adored her.

With Megan's lust for adventure and all things odd, and Dani's natural instincts to follow Megan's lead, it never failed the three would find themselves somewhere weird, and usually in trouble. Tonight would be no exception.

When Dani had suggested Le Club d'Esclavage for their evening entertainment, arousal had been Megan's first response. Although Megan didn't have a burning interest in the BDSM scene, she'd be lying if she didn't admit to being a mite curious. The fact her father had fought tooth and nail to put a kibosh on the club's opening fed her curiosity like gas tossed into an already roaring fire.

As the taxi carried them through town, thoughts of the articles she'd read regarding the club had her shivering with nervous excitement. Megan was aware of the private playrooms located on the club's second floor. She also knew as long as the sexual experience was consensual between the players, anything went.

The words of the club's manager echoed in her mind: "The owner would like to make one thing very clear. When you cross the threshold into Le Club d'Esclavage, it is your desire to participate completely in our manner of play, and such will be expected of you."

The thought of what went on in the risqué club had her pulse racing, and had made her panties damp on more than one occasion. Though curious, and somewhat intrigued, she'd decided there was no way someone was going to tie her up and beat her, just for kicks. Sexual or not.

As they neared the club, Megan wasn't the least bit concerned about what might happen once inside. Hell, it wasn't as if some hunk of man would toss her over his shoulder and cart her off to his dungeon of torture.

She just didn't have that kind of good luck.

Over the past few years, Megan's social life had become almost nonexistent. If it weren't for Nat and Dani, and of course her job, she'd have little reason to even leave her condo. The thought of someone 'choosing' her as their evening playmate tonight was absurd, in her opinion. It had become clear that she gave off the 'stay the hell away' vibe where the opposite sex was concerned.

She'd always been very particular who she shared her body with. Hell, the guy she gave her virginity to when she was twenty five thought her a freak. "Are you fucking kidding," he'd said. "A bitch as fine as you should be well broken in by your age." Their six month relationship ended that night.

She'd grown tired of inept fingers groping, and mouths slobbering all over her. If that was all sex had to offer, she'd gladly go without. It was sad, really. She'd never once achieved climax at the hands of a lover.

Believing the hurtful remarks her ex made about her being frigid, Megan had wandered into an adult novelty shop one day after breaking it off with the jerk, and purchased a vibrator. Sex toy in hand, she quickly realized she hadn't been the one with the problem. By herself, she found sexual release aplenty, yet knew there should be more.

She missed the caress of a lover, whether rough with urgency or tender and unhurried. Megan enjoyed the exchange of dirty talk with a lover—sensual spoken words to further stimulate the senses—but had yet to find a lover who could say the right things at the right moment. Was there something so terribly wrong with a man telling a woman what he wanted her to do sexually, or vise versa? Megan didn't think so. But her experiences so far had shown her that men just took what they needed. If she happened to get off in the act, so be it.

Besides the absence of a warm, muscular male body to hold her, something else was missing. Sure, she was getting off, but it wasn't enough. She knew what she needed was out there, somewhere. Megan desired to be with a man who took charge. Someone who wouldn't hesitate to take what he needed and wanted, yet be attentive and attuned to her needs in return. Megan was prepared and willing to give everything to the right man, but the reward had to work both ways.

At twenty-nine, Megan had convinced herself she'd never find a suitable lover. But she was far from ready to settle for a mediocre one.

Considering where she'd come from, it was no wonder her views of love, sex and relationships were rather deluded.

Coming from old money, Megan had never wanted for anything growing up, except perhaps structured guidance. Barton Washington the Fourth, a successful politician with no time for his family, had always found time for his many mistresses. Marilyn Dubois-Washington, the dutiful, supportive wife with no backbone, had a closet addiction to the bottle. To the outside world they appeared to be the picture perfect, all-American family. Inside the Washington home, however, was a different story.

Megan had learned early on that as long as she towed the line playing the perfect little girl Daddy expected her to be, she wouldn't feel his wrath. He'd never struck her—hell no, that would have required physical contact. The man never had any time for her outside of photo ops and public relation gatherings.

Unbeknownst to those who respected and looked up to him, inside the confines of their home, her father had a temper that would make his constituents wonder what in the hell they ever saw in him. No, in Megan's twenty-nine years her father never raised a hand to her or her mother, but more times than she could remember, they'd been relegated to clean up crew when he'd gone off on a tangent, destroying everything in sight.

In her father's opinion child rearing was the woman's job. He stood firm that he worked damn hard to bring home the bacon. So, it was the responsibility of the woman he'd married to raise his children, and run his home.

Megan always laughed at his campaign stance on 'treating women as equals'. If the public could only see inside the walls of their mansion on the hill…

Due to the farce of her upbringing, Megan always shied away from the high life. Instead she found comfort and support in Natalie and Dani. Through her best friends, she'd learned there was much more to life than money. Money could buy material possessions, but not the things that really mattered most. Emotional fulfillment and the love of her friends meant more to her than anything her father's money could ever buy.

With her father being a political powerhouse, it didn't take Megan long to learn her place as a politician's daughter. Over the years she quickly realized she could have a different date every night of the week if she chose. Yet Megan hadn't dated at all in more than three years. The men her parents insisted she go out with were usually only interested in who her daddy was, and how being with her could further their own agendas.

In a rebellious fit, she'd applied for, and got, a position in a clothing store in the local mall. Her parents were less than pleased. According to her father, her station in life dictated she carry herself accordingly. In their opinion—or her father's, truth be told—her only job be the doting wife and mother, with no valuable opinions of her own. Once she learned her place, a stable, willing man would keep her. When she learned her place, her father reminded her. Repeatedly.

Fat chance!

Megan had always been her own person, and intended to continue living her life as she chose.

Tonight wasn't about her, though, or Dani. Tonight was about helping Natalie reenter the world of the 'living'.

On the drive to the club, she and Dani chatted away while Natalie gazed absently out the window, not paying them any attention at all.

"Okay, Meg." Natalie finally broke into their conversation. "Where are you taking me?" Her expression was one of annoyance. Sitting on either side of Natalie, she and Dani giggled excitedly.

Dani grabbed Natalie's hand and gently kissed the back of it. "Nat, you really need to take a load off. You're going to get all wrinkly before you're thirty if you don't let go of all that stress."

Truth be told, Megan was anxious to work off a little stress herself. All day she looked forward to getting her groove on out on the dance floor. Something told her this night was going to be something sensational.

"Dani's right, Nat. Now that the Marsden project is finished and on its way to print, it's time you let those gorgeous curls down and cut loose! Hell, we haven't spent any time with you since you were assigned that account. So tonight, you are ours."

"Well, for a little while anyway." Dani wagged her brows.

"What the hell is that suppose to mean? Oh God, what are you two up to?" Natalie asked. Apprehension more than clear in her voice.

Neither one offered her an answer.

Five minutes later the taxi rolled to a stop.

"Oooh we're here!" Megan and Dani squealed in unison.

Megan paid the driver and followed Dani and Natalie out of the car. The expression on her friend's pretty face almost made her wet her pants with laughter.

"Oh…my…God," Natalie gasped. "We are not going in there." She stood shaking her head, gaping at Dani and Megan, giggling on either side of her.

Tonight is going to be fun, Megan thought. Just wait until Nat sees the surprise waiting for her inside.

"Damn straight," Megan replied as she and Dani linked their arms with Natalie and headed for the front door, bypassing those waiting in line.

"Hi, Mikey." Dani tipped her head coyly, greeting the large man at the door.

"Good evening, ladies. Welcome to Le Club d'Esclavage," he greeted the threesome and winked directly at Dani.

Natalie spun her head around to look at a moony-eyed Dani and stifled another gasp. "Dani, have you—"

"Maybe once or twice," Dani snickered. "Now come on. Let's get in there."

Dani pulled them through the door Mikey held open. He stopped them short. "I'll meet you in there shortly." He smiled suggestively at Dani as she giggled and they quickly made their entrance.

Natalie threw a speculative glance at her friend, and although Megan's curiosity prickled her skin, Natalie's expression was more than enough for the both of them.

* * * *

Troy Simon stood in front of the antique floor-length mirror, buttoning his black silk shirt. As he blew a dark curl from the middle of his forehead, the door to the adjoining bathroom opened, and his lover Ransom Seager strolled out.

The man was beyond sexy. A fluffy bath towel hung low on slender hips, taut, tanned flesh dewy from his shower. The blond waves atop his head gave him an innocent school boy appearance. From experience, Troy knew the man was anything but. Ransom's celery green eyes could pull the deepest secrets from someone's soul with a subtle glance. The fullness of his lips beckoned to be ravished by a mouth, or fucked by a cock.

It wasn't until their paths had crossed several years earlier that Troy first felt the twinges of attraction toward another man. Something about Ransom drew Troy. Despite his domineering nature, he'd found himself powerless to resist Ransom's charms.

When they'd met, Ransom worked construction, a job he'd taken after his shot as a first round draft pick for the NHL was shattered when he blew out his left knee in college. Though injured ten years earlier, he still walked with a slight limp when he'd done too much on his feet. Due to his love of the sport, Ransom now coached Pee Wee Hockey, and had landed a position in the office of the construction firm designing buildings.

Ransom's company had been awarded the contract to build Le Club d'Esclavage, and due to his diligence, they'd opened weeks ahead of the projected schedule.

The more time he spent with Ransom, the more he realized they were meant to be. Not only was the man the most compatible and fulfilling sexual partner he'd ever been with, Ransom completed Troy on a spiritual and emotional level as well. They weren't just buddies, or lovers, they'd become the best of friends.

Whether they were working, or playing Troy never tired of watching Ransom. The man moved with the grace and ease of a jungle cat. He exuded confidence and power, and hid it all behind a playful grin of innocence.

Troy felt as though he were the luckiest man on the face of the earth. Theirs was a relationship of stability and comfort, and most importantly, unconditional acceptance. Tonight, if things played out as they'd both hoped and half-assed planned, their lives were about to take a turn in a different direction. One equally as fulfilling as the path they traveled now, but in the end, there would be three.

As much as he enjoyed keeping his lover all to himself, Troy desired to watch his lover with another. Perhaps a residual kink from his days of training others interested in getting in touch with their dominant sexual sides.

In the height of enjoying the lifestyle, several friends and strangers alike requested his guidance and tutelage exploring the BDSM world. Bondage, the use of toys and implements and pain within reason were completely acceptable modes of play. Ones Troy highly encouraged, and participated in himself.

In the day, nothing turned him on like watching others engaging in coupling. The expressions which crossed a woman's face as her lover brought her to climax could make Troy come without even touching himself.

There were those who liked to watch and those who liked to be watched. Troy could be classed in either category.

Since he and Ransom decided to put this evening's plan into motion, Troy enjoyed mental visions of his lover driving himself into the tight heat of a woman's body. But not just any woman. They had someone special in mind. Bending her over a bar stool, or laying her out across the pool table. And after getting his fill of playing voyeur, he would get in on the action.

Troy was about to unload now just thinking about the experience, and the woman they would be sharing.

Ransom, finally feeling the weight of Troy's gaze, glanced up. With a playful grin, he hitched his chin at him.

Troy reached for the solid length between his legs, as it now ached.

"I don't want you wore out before the evening festivities," Ransom chided.

"No worries there," Troy assured him. "I'll be more than ready, willing and able to perform, and be entertained."

With slow confident steps Ransom closed the distance between them and replaced Troy's hand with his own. Leaning in, he pressed his lips to Troy's, slipping his tongue between when Troy opened for him.

Troy reached for the towel covering his lover, snatched it off, dropping it on the floor. His hand skimmed across the tensing muscles of Ransom's sculpted chest to pinch one tight, puckered nipple, then the other.

"How about a little something to take the edge off, babe." Ransom grinned. Dropping to his knees, he worked Troy's belt, snap and zipper free, and slid his leather pants down his hips.

* * * *

For the second time that evening Troy stood in front of the mirror, straightening his clothes. Despite the satisfying release his lover brought him, Troy was still sexually frustrated. Across the room, Ransom tugged a t-shirt over his head, and pulled a pair of faded denim over his slender hips.

"So, everything is in place then?" Ransom asked, racking his fingers through his blond waves.

"Haven't heard any different," Troy replied. After a few moments of silence he turned toward his lover. "Are you certain this is what you want?"

Ransom's face blanched for a split second before regaining his composure. "Are you having second thoughts?"

Troy shook his head, his nerves eating at his insides. No, he wasn't having second thoughts. He wanted this more than he'd ever wanted anything before. "I feel as though maybe I talked you into it."

Ransom chuckled. "That's never stopped you before, Master."

Troy's balls pulsed behind supple leather at Ransom calling him 'Master'. He loved hearing the endearing term spoken from his lover's lips. Though they shared a Master/slave relationship in their sexual relations, they generally left it in the playroom. The times it slipped into regular conversation caught Troy unawares, and tended to ignite his libido.

There had been one occasion in his past where Troy entertained a 24/7 arrangement, but he quickly discovered it wasn't what he wanted in a permanent relationship. He didn't want or need someone catering to his every whim, every moment of the day. Nor did he desire the responsibility that went along with it. He wanted someone to dominate sexually. It was as simple as that. In all other aspects of a relationship, he and his partner would be equals.

He'd found the person he needed and wanted in Ransom.

"This is a big deal, Ransom, and it has to be a decision that is mutually agreed upon."

Taking a few steps forward, Ransom wrapped his fingers around Troy's upper arms and gave a firm squeeze. "Rest assured, babe, my eyes are wide open. It's been a long time since I've been with a woman, but I think I still remember how to please one," he teased.

"Stop fucking around," Troy snipped. "This is serious."

"What's gotten into you?" Ransom asked. A concerned frown creased his brow. "All right, listen, if you aren't ready or think maybe this isn't something you truly want, I'll understand. Things are already in motion, so we need to be on the same page before we walk out that door tonight."

Troy threw his head back and drew in a deep breath. He allowed the silence between them as a time to collect his thoughts.

"You're right," he said.

"I usually am," Ransom countered.

"Such a smartass."

"Yeah, I know. Now let's get a move on, stud. Dani wouldn't let us down, Troy," Ransom said, releasing his hold on Troy's arms. "And after what the three of us have shared over the past few weeks, we shouldn't let her down either."

CHAPTER 2

Inside the club the bass from the dance music vibrated through her body. Glancing around the vast open area, Megan felt the energy of life pulsing within. The bodies gyrating on the dance floor moved as one in time to the throbbing bass. The majority of the patrons were scarcely dressed, displaying more than enough tits and ass to last her a lifetime.

Megan wasn't a prude, but did feel out of her element now inside the club. When Dani first suggested it, spending the evening at Le Club d'Esclavage had seemed like a great idea. However, now that she was inside watching the near-naked patrons, Megan wondered why in the hell she'd allowed Dani to talk her into coming here.

This is for Nat and Max, Megan reminded herself. She was going to help her best friend see that her true love worked in the office just down the hall from her.

In a few minutes Megan found herself moving to the beat of the dance music. A familiar song vibrated around the room and she began moving in time to the thrumming.

"This is awesome," she said, leaning between Natalie and Dani.

"I told you so," Dani snickered, and started dancing with Megan as the trio made their way toward the bar.

For an hour or so the girls continued to dance and chit-chat, and Megan found herself actually enjoying the atmosphere of the club.

As they stood with their backs to the dance floor, a hulking shadow blocked out the flashing lights. When they all spun around, Dani's expression tightened as she met the heated gaze of Mikey, the doorman.

Mike was tall with broad shoulders, and towered over Dani's petite frame. His domineering presence didn't seem to faze her at all.

"Are you finished for the night?" she asked evenly, her tone a complete opposite to the one she used with him a short time earlier.

"I'm all yours, my Mistress," he replied,

Mistress? Megan thought. Just as she was about to question Dani, her friend reached up and grabbed the silk tie dangling from Mike's neck, and gave a light tug.

"Enjoy your evening, ladies," he said to Megan and Natalie as he followed behind Dani.

Megan exchanged a look of 'what the fuck' with Natalie. Both replied to each other with a shrug.

"So, you having fun, Nat?"

Natalie smiled, but Megan knew her heart wasn't in it. It was okay. Max would arrive soon enough, and that alone would put a smile on her friend's face.

A comfortable silence settled between them, and Megan took to people watching. Glancing at the crowd to her left, she spotted a god seated on the other side of the bar looking in her direction. Megan grinned back, and casually peeked over her shoulder. When she turned back, his eyes were still focused on her.

Feeling a tad self-conscious under his scrutiny, she smoothed her hands down the torso of her blouse, and then pointed a finger to the center of her chest.

'Me' she mouthed.

He nodded, and flashed a smile so laced with sex she was positive she creamed her panties.

This night is getting even better, she mused to herself.

The soft notes of Natalie's voice were barely audible over the sound of the music. The visions suddenly in the forefront of Megan's mind were of the handsome stranger tying her to his bed, and then...

A chill raced up her spine and she shivered.

"Are you even listening to me?"

Megan reluctantly turned her attention toward her friend. She felt terrible for ignoring Natalie, but she just couldn't take her eyes or her mind off the man across the bar.

As Megan opened her mouth to apologize, Natalie piped up, "Oh fuck it, just go."

Megan sat stunned for a moment, and then seized the opportunity.

"Oooh, you're the best! I love you!" Meg squealed and kissed Natalie's cheek. "Have fun! See you later!"

Unable to resist the pull of the man's gaze, Megan approached the handsome stranger at the bar, her body warm and tingly. She attempted to tamp the carnal thoughts swimming around in her mind, and then thought, 'Hey what the hell, I'm a big girl'.

Never before had she the desire to engage a stranger in a bar. There was something about the man that seemed to draw her.

"Hello," she said. The huskiness in her tone sent warmth to the juncture between her thighs.

His sexy smile made her nipples tighten, almost painfully. The clean scent of subtle cologne exuded masculinity.

"What's a pretty lady like you doing in a club like this?" he asked, in a low sultry voice.

Megan reached for the edge of the bar for balance when her knees threatened to give out. The deep, smoky timbre caressed over her like the touch of a lover.

"Bad cliché, huh?" His chuckle was nearly enough to finish her off.

"Yeah a little. But it's all right," she snickered. "Like everyone else, I'm just looking for a good time," she heard herself saying in a tone sounding a lot like a come-on.

The blond grinned, giving her a thorough visual once-over. Her insides heated as his eyes traveled inch by inch over her body.

"Then you've come to the right place," he declared with a confidence that curled Megan's toes. "I'm certain I can help you with that. My name is Ransom."

"Megan," she replied, and shook his proffered hand. "And is that so? You showing me a good time?" she asked, batting her long dark eyelashes at him.

"Oh yeah. May I get you a drink?"

"I've already had a couple of drink-drinks, so a soda would be great for now. Thank you."

Ransom gained the attention of the petite woman behind the bar, and ordered two virgin cocktails.

The close proximity of the handsome stranger made her belly flutter and her palms sweaty. Megan couldn't recall any past experience where a man simply looking at her had turned her insides out. As they conversed, she found herself wondering what he would taste like. His skin, his mouth, his… What would his hands feel like as they explored her naked form? Would he be a rough or a gentle lover? She found herself wondering just what sort of heat Ransom was packing inside the lucky denim hugging his lower body.

After a couple of hours, Megan was surprised her comfort level had grown considerably toward Ransom. A little voice in her mind told her to go for it.

"So, when I first saw you, you were sitting with a friend. Girls' night out?" he asked.

Megan giggled. "Yeah, sort of. Natalie, the girl I was with, has the hots for her coworker, Max. Max has the hots for Nat. But the two of them can't seem to get their shit together and hook up. So Max approached our friend Dani a few weeks ago for some help in getting him and Nat in the same place together. One of them suggested this place, I don't know which one, and the rest is history. I saw Max with Nat earlier," Megan said, and scanned the crowd mingling around the bar. "But it looks like they're gone now. Oh well, I know she's in good hands."

"And how about you?" he asked. "Do you feel as though you're in good hands?"

A shudder jolted through Megan, and she knew Ransom saw her body's reaction. She had no control over the trembling of her body, at the sensual tone lacing his words. If her nipples distended any further, they were going to explode right through the thin fibers of her blouse, leaving two tiny little holes in the material.

"Time will tell," she heard herself respond, her breathless tone carried an invitation.

"Excellent call coming here then. I'm certain you will have the time of your life tonight," he said, his blue eyes sparkling with mischief.

Reminding herself it had been so long since she'd felt the warmth of a man's body against hers, she decided to give tonight everything she had. Her sex life up until now had been abysmal to say the least, but she'd never before been in the company of someone like Ransom.

He exuded sex, confidence and power. And Megan had little doubt he knew exactly what buttons to push to help a woman achieve ultimate pleasure.

Hell, what have you got to lose, Meg? the voice asked her. It's not like anyone else is ringing your bell, or ever has.

Inwardly, Megan cringed. The subconscious was correct. The only orgasms she experienced were ones she brought herself to.

As Ransom's eyes flickered with interest and promise, Megan realized she'd closed the short space between them. He didn't stop her when she slid her leg between his thighs, and stroked a finger tip along his bare forearm.

As if reading her mind, he leaned down, bringing his mouth close to her ear. The warmth of his breath caressed her cheek and neck, and her pussy grew wet. Ransom placed a hand on her waist, the heat of his touch a firebrand through the fabric of her blouse. Slowly his hand roamed up the length of her torso, his thumb brushing the side of her right breast.

"Will you allow me to take you someplace a little more private, my sweet Meg?" he asked.

Megan's head nodded by itself, and her body began to tingle.

"I've something very special planned for you," he promised. "Come," he said, taking her hand in his, and led her through the grinding bodies on the dance floor.

* * * *

On the way up the flight of stairs it was all Ransom could do to stop himself from pinning the woman following him up against the wall and ravishing her.

That was not part of the plan, though.

The throb between his legs was becoming hard to ignore, and now he wished he'd strapped a cock ring around his organ before leaving the apartment. But then, in his own defense, he hadn't expected Megan to send his body skyrocketing so easily.

When she'd met his gaze earlier, she'd looked back at him with interest, intrigue and willingness. The willingness was what he searched for, and he didn't have to look very hard. Dani had been right: her friend was a natural sexual submissive, and now she would be his. Troy's and his. And together they would show her just how fulfilling the life of a sub could be.

During the 'sessions' with Dani over the past few weeks Ransom had confessed to his lover that a woman to share would be a welcome addition to their relationship.

Troy was in complete agreement.

When Dani discussed Megan with them, neither man could believe their good fortune. Megan Washington sounded like their perfect complement.

The honey blond of her hair reminded Ransom of rippling wheat in a field. There was a sensuality simmering in the depths of her chocolate brown eyes, and Ransom was already picturing her looking up at him from between his thighs. As he spoke to her, he could have sworn he could already feel the fullness of her plump lips wrapped tight around the girth of his shaft.

Megan possessed curves which should have been outlawed. She was one hundred percent woman, voluptuous, buxom, and shapely in all the right places. He saw himself bending her at the waist, grabbing hold of her rounded hips, and sliding himself as deep as he could go. Ransom wanted nothing more than to lose himself inside her, and to take his lover along for the ride.

Then there would be the taste of her. He'd enjoyed the feminine scent of her skin when he'd leaned in to whisper in her ear. He knew once he slipped his tongue inside her, he would be at her mercy.

As they made their way down the corridor to his and Troy's apartment, Ransom chuckled to himself.

Before they made their exit, he'd spied Troy studying them. Despite the blowjob he'd given his lover earlier, Ransom knew the sight of Megan had Troy's cock standing at full attention, just like his own. He'd seen the flames of desire flickering in his lover's eyes.

Upon entering the suite, Ransom gave into his need. He had to sample her. As he turned and pushed the door closed behind them, he backed Megan against the wall, and lowered his mouth to hers. With gentle persistence he urged her to part her lips for him. Her taste was just as he'd suspected it would be. Pure, innocent, feminine.

In her fists, she gripped his t-shirt as if holding on for dear life.

Soft womanly moans were captured by his exploring lips and tongue. It was then Ransom scented her arousal in the air between them.

Pulling back, he stared into her eyes, seeing his reflection along with need and desire.

"Will you put your implicit trust in me, my precious Megan?" he asked. "Will you allow me complete control to see to your pleasure?"

Though she hesitated to answer, desire and curiosity continued to flicker in her gaze.

"Let me show you what I have in mind. All right?"

This time she nodded. Taking her hand, Ransom led her across the living room and through a large set of double doors, where they entered the playroom.

When he flicked the switch beside the door, several lights came to life, casting dim light around the room.

* * * *

Megan gasped at the sight before her.

Ransom's hand pressed against the small of her back, urging her to step forward. A soft click announced the closing of the door.

Apparatuses and devises reminding Megan of things used to torture people in medieval times were arranged around the large room. The pungent aroma of leather tickled her nose.

"I assure you, baby," he whispered close to her ear from behind. "Nothing will happen without your complete consent."

Though intrigued, and very aroused, Megan was apprehensive. In silence she stepped forward toward the various benches and stands. Restraints dangled in diffcrent places from above and close to the ground.

Displayed on the shelves lining the walls were items Megan had never seen before. On one she spied an assortment of toys resembling her vibrator tucked in the top drawer of her nightstand. Instead of being cylindrical in their total design, they had flared bases, and two had multiple nodules in ascending sizes along their length.

As she stared at the toys she felt the heat of Ransom's stare.

"Butt plugs," he said quietly.

"P-pardon?" She spun around, startled to find him standing directly behind her.

He reached past her and took a medium-sized one off the shelf. "These are an assortment of butt plugs."

"You mean, people stick them…" Her cheeks caught fire, and the tiny knot of nerves between her legs began to pulse.

"They are inserted into the rectum to prepare one for anal sex," he said.

"Does it… I mean, do they hurt?"

"Not when administered properly. We would begin with a small one, and when you were comfortable with that, we'd move up in size until you were stretched enough to accept a cock."

"What do you mean me?" Megan gasped. Nothing was going in

her backside.

Ransom's sexy chuckle made her nipples tighten. "I was speaking in general terms. As I told you a minute ago, nothing will be done without your consent."

"Are you going to hurt me?" she asked, and although feeling unprepared for his answer, she took a step toward him.

"No, Megan."

That was an instant relief. The scent of him had Megan stepping closer.

"Do you…want to hurt me?" she asked, studying his unfaltering expression.

"No, baby. I just want to show you pleasures you've never imagined," he said. "Have you ever experienced a bit of pain with your pleasure?"

Megan shook her head. "To be honest, Ransom, I've never felt pleasure at the hands of someone else."

His sexy smile broadened. "Then you are most definitely in the right hands. I can make you feel so good…"

His sentence trailed off as he pulled Megan against him and pressed his lips to hers. Her knees threatened to give out as his tongue slipped past her lips. The taste of this man set her on the cusp of spontaneous combustion.

When he pulled back, Megan whimpered, "Show me."

Ransom's smile melted away the last of her control.

"That's my girl. Let's start by getting you out of these clothes," he kept his voice soft, like a caress, and reached for the buttons of her blouse. Slowly he worked them loose, and pushed the flimsy fabric off her shoulders, down her arms, and to the floor.

Strong hands stroked up the length of her arms, the contact of his skin along hers electric.

"You are beautiful, Meg. So beautiful. Now," he said and lowered himself to one knee. "Let me see if your panties match your pretty bra."

Ransom leaned forward, pressing his lips to her midriff, placing gentle kisses along the waist of her leather miniskirt. Around to her back his hands roamed. They smoothed over the supple material, and then cupped her rear in their palms.

Megan moaned, dropping her head forward, her eyes squeezed shut. Needing to touch him, her fingers raked through his blond waves, fisting and releasing, holding his mouth to her.

The sound of her zipper descending carried in the silence around them.

Ransom's touch was magical. Megan hadn't even realized the leather was pooled at her feet until his voice pulled her back into reality.

"Step out, baby."

She did, and when her heel slipped off, he pushed it back on.

"Let's leave the heels on, shall we? They're very sexy," he said.

Blushing, Megan nodded, and took a single step backward.

Ransom's eyes caressed every inch of her body, singeing her flesh with each pass. Before him she stood in bra and panties, thigh-high stockings with lace trim around the top, and heels.

The vision she pictured of herself was that of a starlet in a porn flick. At that moment, Megan didn't care. The man on his knees looked at her like she was the only woman on the face of the earth.

"W-will you tie me up?" she asked tentatively, and with eager anticipation. Did she really want Ransom to bind her, rendering her helpless?

"I would love to, baby. Come over here," he said getting to his feet and taking her hand.

He led Megan to an apparatus which resembled a giant X. Turning her back to the center support, he placed a kiss on her mouth.

"Before we go any further, you need a safe word," Ransom said.

Megan blinked in confusion, and then stammered, "A safe word?"

"Yes. It's a word for you to speak if what we do becomes too much for you to handle. It's a word that will make us stop immediately because you are uncomfortable with what we are doing."

"Why can't I just say stop?"

The smokiness of his deep chuckle, moved through Megan like molten lava.

"Because people sometimes say things they don't mean in the

throes of passion. Like 'no' when they mean 'yes', or 'stop', and then pray their lover won't."

"Oh. Okay."

"Now choose a word that you will remember, and be able to speak if you need to, no matter what is happening," he said.

"Apple sauce," she blurted out. Where in the hell did that come from?

Ransom smiled wide, but didn't comment.

"It's the first thing to come to my mind," she said with a shrug.

"Apple sauce it is, baby. Are you ready?"

Megan nodded.

"From here on out, you must answer with words. Understand?"

"Yes. I am ready," she said.

"That's my girl."

* * * *

Troy Simon took the stairs two at a time toward his suite on the third level of the building, which housed the personal living quarters of a few of the staff.

The grin curling his lips brought back memories of an afternoon in junior high, when he and his best friend Davey got caught peeking into the girls' locker room.

For the first time since reaching puberty, Troy found himself on the brink of losing control of his libido. It had been a long time since a woman brought his body to total attention with just a smile. Hell, she hadn't even made eye contact with him. It had been her animated interaction with Ransom alone that stimulated him in all the right places.

The sight of Ransom speaking with Megan at the bar now had Troy's balls pulsing like never before. Despite him and his lover going "both ways", during their five year commitment neither had ever expressed a desire to bring a third into their relationship. Let alone a woman.

The waves of Megan's long sandy blond hair reminded him of strands of silk. Big brown eyes may have hidden a deep, dark secret from someone untrained to spot it, but Troy recognized it. Restrained passion. If he were to wager a guess based on the glimmer he saw, he suspected she repressed her sexual appetite. That was because Megan had yet to find the right men.

Written all over her delicate features, Troy read sub. Under the right circumstances, the beauty would give herself to a suitable Master, completely. Pausing outside the sound proof steel door to the playroom in his suite, Troy drew a deep breath, hopeful he would be awarded the opportunity to test the woman's sexual limits. If all went well with his lover…

Giving the knob a turn, he pushed open the door and his breath caught in his throat. Flames from dozens of lit candles flickered, creating a warm glow about the room. Combined fragrances of vanilla, musk and feminine arousal scented the air.

In the center of the room bound hand and foot to a St. Andrews Cross, was Megan Washington. Blindfolded, clad in a skimpy pair of violet panties with matching bra, stockings, and heels. She looked simply delectable.

Though several yards separated them, Troy caught her fragrance in the air, and he momentarily savored the sight of her heaving bosom. The sound of harsh breath told him she hadn't heard him enter.

Or perhaps she had.

On the ground to Megan's left Ransom knelt. The firm cheeks of his ass seated on his heels, knees slightly spread, hands rested palms up on the tops of his thighs, eyes lowered. Jutting proudly from between his powerful legs, his smooth, long, thick cock pulsed. Despite the distance, Troy's mouth watered as a drop of pre-cum trickled from the slit at the end.

His lover had done well.

"Well, what do we have here?" Troy said and pushed the door closed behind him.

The sensual gasp of surprise slipping from Megan's full lips sent a shiver up the length of Troy's spine.

Troy delighted in the stiffening of her body as Ransom answered.

"I've brought you a present, Master."

CHAPTER 3

"So I see," Troy replied drawing closer toward the pair.

His pulse raced, and the bead of sweat running down his lower back made him shiver.

"But, I—"

Troy cut her words off by pressing a fingertip against her trembling lips.

"Now am I to understand, slave, that I am to enjoy two playthings this evening?" Troy began and stroked a single digit from his other hand from the waistband of Megan's panties to just under her left breast. "Or is this pretty package a toy for two?"

"You know me too well, Master," Ransom replied, eyes still focused on the floor.

Removing his finger away from her quivering lips, Troy gently pushed a lock of hair behind her ear. Beneath his touch her body trembled. Feeding his hunger all the more.

"She is very lovely, slave," Troy continued, and leaned into her.

Tighter her body coiled, yet the fragrance of her arousal became stronger.

Recognizing her waver, the Dom in him came forth, needing to push her past the limits of her comfort zone. Reaching out, he cupped her pussy with his left hand. The suddenness of his action and the persistent pressure used brought Megan to her tiptoes.

"Yes, Master," Ransom said in agreement.

"My pretty slave girl, your panties are wet already, and we've barely begun," Troy commented, pressing his middle finger against the heat of her center.

She gasped again struggling against the restraints.

"Wh-what are you d-doing?" she stammered. "Th-this isn't what I h-had in m-m-mind."

Troy leaned closer still, and after nipping the lobe of her ear, whispered, "You have your safe word?" He knew she did. Ransom scrawled the word applesauce on the notepad beside the door where he would see it before entering the playroom.

After a handful of seconds, she nodded.

"Would you like to speak it?"

Without hesitation she shook her head from side to side. "But, I—
"

"Silence," Troy said in an authoritative tone. "Your safe word is the only thing that will put a stop to our play. You entered the doors of this club of your own accord, my pretty, did you not?"

Again Megan nodded.

"Therefore," Troy said in a softer tone, and then pressed his lips to hers in a tender kiss. "You are mine until I say we are finished. Do you understand?"

A jerky nod was her reply.

"Very well. Rise, slave, and rid our new toy of the fabric hiding her from us."

When Ransom stood, Troy wrapped his hand around the back of his neck and pulled his mouth to his own. After thoroughly exploring each other, they pulled back and smiled. The simmering desire he found in his lover's eyes tested his control.

"You've done well," he said

"Thank you, Master," Ransom replied.

"And for being such a thoughtful, slave, I'm going to share my gift with you."

Ransom smiled the sexy grin that Troy had fallen in love with five years earlier.

"Thank you, Master."

After leaning in for another kiss, Ransom turned and crossed the room toward a chest of drawers. Retrieving what he sought, he came back and stood in front of Megan.

She inhaled a sharp breath as the cold metal of the scissors in Ransom's hand slid under the hem of her bra between her breasts. Her

[94]

body began to tremble.

With a snip, the lacy material rended and her breasts spilled free.

"So very beautiful," Troy said, reaching out to cup the ampleness of the left one.

Megan's breath quickened, and he could see the pulse in her neck beat at a rapid pace.

Dipping his head he licked the flat of his tongue over the rigid tip. His cock throbbed in his pants, an ache he wasn't sure he'd ever experienced in the past. In his left hand he massaged her right breast, turning his oral attention there.

Beneath his touch Megan's body stiffened and relaxed as he experimented with various pressures and techniques. Harder, then softer, he suckled. Gentle nibbles, followed by sharp nips made her cry out.

When her hips began to grind against him, Troy withdrew his touch and backed away.

Reaching between his legs he rubbed his cock, trying to sooth the vicious ache he felt there. His breath was harsh, raspy, and he neared the brink of being uncontrolled.

"The panties," he ordered hoarsely.

The heated desire burning in Ransom's eyes when their gazes met reflected his own, of that he was certain. Being lovers as long as they had, Ransom was well aware of Troy's limitations. And the grin he flashed him told Troy his lover knew his control was being tested.

"The panties, Master," he repeated, slipped the scissors along Megan's left hip, and cut. "Can you smell her sweet pussy, Master?"

"Yes," Troy croaked, knowing Ransom was baiting him in play. Well, two could play that game. "Would you like to be the first to taste her, slave?" Troy asked as the second cut sliced through the lace and silk fabric on the right side.

Ransom attempted to stifle a groan as the material fell to the floor from between Megan's legs.

"Oh God," she whispered.

What a sight she made. Bound hand and foot, blindfolded, her bra cut through the middle, straps hanging loosely on her shoulders, large, beautiful breasts heaving as she struggled for breath. Between her legs, the lips of her pussy were bare and glistening with her arousal.

Troy took several deep breaths of his own to squelch his desire. It did him no good. He was going to shoot his load in his leather pants, just watching the woman helplessly restrained before him.

"You are so fucking beautiful, Megan," he declared through a ragged breath.

Beside him, Ransom's body was peppered in a light sheen of sweat. Troy knew he fought to maintain his composure. The fat crown of his cock pulsed, angry purple in color, droplets of pre-cum flowing freely from the tip.

"Taste her," Troy commanded.

Ransom dropped to his knees, and buried his face between

[96]

Megan's legs.

Megan cried out, sinking her teeth into her lower lip.

Troy reached a hand out to massage one breast, then the other. With his free hand, he unzipped his pants and pulled his cock free. Wrapping his fingers around his length he stroked himself, savoring the sight before him.

Megan's cries grew desperate, her hips thrusting against Ransom's mouth as best she could with his hands holding her still. From side to side she tossed her head, the scent of her arousal announcing the pending release.

"Do not come, slave girl," Troy ordered her.

Whimpering a valiant protest she arched her back, pressing her breast into his hand.

"P-please," she begged.

"Not until I say you can," he reiterated in a firmer tone.

"I-I can't…" she sobbed.

Troy waited several seconds before uttering a command. "Enough, slave," he said, and pulled his hand away from her breasts. At his feet Ransom sat back from Megan, both of them gasping for much needed air.

"Calm yourself, Megan," Troy groaned through his own calming technique. "Fight back your need to come."

She continued to take slow, deep breaths, her body trembling, clamoring for release.

Troy leaned over and using his finger under Ransom's chin, tipped his head up. His lips and chin were wet with Megan's essence. A look of determination flickered in his green eyes.

"You look as though you enjoyed her, slave," Troy stated the obvious with a grin.

"Yes, Master, very much. Our new toy is sweet, her taste addictive. May I have more?"

"Not yet. I want to sample her on your lips," Troy growled, and captured his lover's mouth in a fierce kiss.

Ransom was right, Megan's juice was delicious. Troy's head began to spin as he worked to clean her nectar from his lover's face. Fisting his fingers in Ransom's hair, Troy allowed himself one last taste before pulling away.

"Have you set a plug?" Troy asked, shooting a glance toward Megan, whose breathing was still ragged. He noticed her nipples harden considerably at the mention of the anal toy.

"No, Master," Ransom replied.

"Start with a medium," Troy ordered, and began unbuttoning his silk shirt. "I want her ready to take me, and soon." A soft feminine gasp drew his attention, and he smiled.

"Yes, Master."

Troy approached the woman bound before him and leaned down, pressing his lips to hers. With eagerness her mouth worked against him, her tongue fighting with his to dominate their oral exchange. He allowed her the moment.

From behind her Ransom appeared, a vibrant pink butt plug in one hand, tube of lubricant in the other. Troy caressed Megan's curves, savoring the silky smoothness of her flesh under his hands. She was perfect, so utterly perfect.

When he pulled his mouth from hers, she whimpered a protest.

"Fingers first," Troy told Ransom, over Megan's shoulder.

"Yes, Master."

Troy watched as Ransom lubed his long, think index finger. Stroking down the length of her body, Troy's hands cupped her buttocks and spread them open. Ransom dropped to his knees, and grinned up at Troy.

When his eyes focused on the backside open to him, Ransom groaned. "What a very pretty pucker, Master," he said.

Megan gasped, and then her breath caught as Ransom slipped his finger in. From above, Troy could see the slow movement of his arm as he slid the digit in and out.

"Your new toy has a nice tight hole, Master," Ransom said, in sultry voice. "You will enjoy fucking her here."

A weak moan escaped past Megan's lips.

After a moment Troy ordered a second finger. Several times he stole kisses from her gapping mouth as Ransom continued to stretch her. Sweat peppered her upper lip and forehead. Troy was near ready to explode as he watched her mouth move, but no sound emitted.

"Now the plug," he said, and Ransom pulled his fingers free. "But first we need to take off the blindfold. I want to look into your eyes as my slave slides the plug up inside your snug ass hole."

Troy released her buttocks, messaging and caressing the globes before stroking his hands up her torso to cup Megan's breasts. He dipped his head to lave them with his tongue. Under his ministrations her body stiffened and she tugged her wrists against the restraints binding her.

Reaching up, Troy lifted the blindfold from Megan's face, watching as she blinked several times acclimating to the sudden light.

* * * *

Wide eyed, Megan looked up at him for a brief moment before dropping her gaze to his chest. Her cheeks caught fire, and her knees threatened to buckle.

The man before her was none other than Troy Simon, the club manager.

Until now she'd only seen pictures of him in magazines, yet was well aware of the reputation his name carried in the world of domination and submission. Now here she stood in front of him, naked, helpless, and bound for his enjoyment.

As her eyes lowered, she realized he too was naked. She attempted to avert her eyes, to no avail. Troy's finger caught her under her chin, lifting her head so she had to choice but to look at him.

Hypnotic gray eyes pierced into her soul.

The man himself, in the flesh, was stunning. Shoulder length, tousled dark brown curls beckoned her touch. Chiseled features denoted power, control, assurance, mastery.

Her body began to tremble under the weight of his stare.

The heat in his gaze sent her heart racing, making her erogenous zones throb. Seconds before, when she realized who'd been touching her, kissing her, she'd been startled. Yet now, reflected in the eyes of the man before her, she felt safe, protected. Desired.

In that instant Megan realized this is what was missing from her life. Not just Troy Simon, but his lover Ransom Seager, as well. To be dominated.

How was it possible to be attracted to two men? she wondered. She was so very confused.

"The plug," Troy repeated, and moved in close.

The stroke of his hands sliding over her skin had her moaning with need.

"Yes," she whimpered, and closed her eyes, reveling in his caress.

In the palm of his hands he gripped the cheeks of her ass, again separating them. The moment something cool and wet touched the sensitive entrance of her butt she tensed, and Troy spoke.

"Look at me," he ordered. "I want to watch every expression that crosses your lovely face as that plug slides in your ass."

Her lower lip quivered with anticipation, and curiosity.

"Will it hurt?" she asked, barely above a whisper.

"It will sting at first," he replied, holding her gaze.

Something blunt penetrated her anus. She stiffened at the foreign intrusion, but Ransom continued to shove the toy inside her.

Megan gasped and groaned, and began to struggle against the restraints binding her.

Troy wasn't kidding about the sting.

"Relax," he encouraged in a soothing tone, and she did.

His eyes continued to hold hers. Need, desire and reassurance brought her peace.

"Take a deep breath, sweetheart," Megan heard from behind.

The stinging turned into a sharp splinter of pain as she sucked in a breath and held it.

"Good girl," the two men praised her in unison.

Blowing out the breath she'd been holding, her body trembled. "I pleased you?" she asked, hopeful. She couldn't control her breathing, and her heart raced. The pleasurable discomfort in her backside added to her growing arousal as Troy's eyes remained focused on her face.

The pad of his thumb rubbed across her lower lip, and she stuck her tongue out to taste him.

"Very much," Troy replied.

With a grin, he slipped his length of his thumb inside her mouth.

Closing her lips around the digit, Megan's lids lowered and she savored his flavor on her tongue.

She needed more.

"You are putting my control to the test, baby," Troy said, his voice hoarse.

Below, the soft clanging of metal buckles dropping to the floor announced the release of her ankles. Gentle, warm hands began to stroke her from her feet, up the length of her legs, to dip between. Higher they climbed, to cup her breasts. From behind, Ransom nibbled along her left shoulder, and nuzzled her neck.

"You accepted the plug with ease, baby," he whispered against her flesh. "How does it feel?"

"B-burning," she answered, releasing Troy's thumb from her lips.

"Find the pleasure," Ransom said. "It's there, seek it out."

Speechless, she focused on the pressure in her derrière, and warmth filled her. As the burning subsided, the tight ring of muscles squeezed the toy, sending jolts of need coursing through her system. As she concentrated on the new sensations stimulating her senses, she realized her vaginal muscles pulsed in time with her anus, and the inside of her thighs grew slick.

Remembering Troy's statement that she wasn't allowed to come, she drew deep breaths to bring her arousal in check.

"The plug will stay in your ass for a little while," Troy announced. "And then we'll swap it for one a little larger."

Megan nodded, her pulse skyrocketing at the promise in his voice.

"Say the words," Ransom reminded her.

"Y-yes."

"Yes, Master," Ransom whispered in her ear.

A chill raced the length of her spine.

"Y-yes, M-Master," she repeated.

Fire flashed in Troy's eyes.

"We're going to untie you now, because I want to feel those sexy, full lips of yours wrapped around my cock," Troy said, reaching for the strap binding her right wrist.

Once freed, he brought her hand to his mouth and placed kisses on her palm and wrist. Ransom tended to the strap on the left.

With her hand still in his, Troy took a few steps backward, putting some space between her and the cross.

"Now you will pleasure me with that sweet, sensual mouth of yours," Troy said, and Megan's heart leapt into her throat. "On your knees," he ordered, and released her hand.

To the floor she dropped, more than eager to do as he asked. From the moment Megan heard his voice when he entered the room, she felt a burning desire to please him.

To please them.

On her knees, the thickest, longest cock she'd ever seen bobbed an inch from her lips. Her mouth watered to sample the solid flesh.

Muskiness tickled her nostrils, feeding her arousal. As she shifted, Megan became more aware of the plug in her ass, and a strangled moan caught her unawares.

Reaching up to touch Troy's length, he stopped her with his voice alone.

"No hands. Only your mouth."

From behind, Ransom's body pressed against her back, and he urged her head forward, though Megan required very little encouragement. With lips open, her tongue slid along the underside of Troy's shaft, taking him into her mouth.

Closing her eyes, Megan inhaled his pungent musk deeply, and closed her lips around him. The taste of him made her head spin. Power, she groaned in silence. Moisture flooded the apex of her thighs, and her body began to ache.

"Very nice," Ransom said taking her hands in his, laying them palm up atop her thighs.

The position of submission he placed her in brought Megan an immediate sense of contentment. The control they possessed over her elated Megan as opposed to demeaning her.

Megan pulled back slowly, prolonging the exquisite sensation of him filling her mouth.

Ransom's hands began caressing and stroking over her heated flesh, fueling the need inside Megan. As she worked Troy's shaft with her mouth her hips took on a mind of their own, grinding her ass against Ransom groin firmly cushioned against her from behind. His hands cupped her breasts, finger tips tugging on her nipples while Troy's hands fisted in her hair.

"Hold still, baby," Troy grunted. "Let me fuck your mouth."

Ransom's arms tightened around Megan, and as Troy plunged deeper, gentle words and soothing tone encouraged her. "Breathe through your nose, and relax your throat," he said, massaging her breasts in the palms of his hands.

It was then Megan realized she needed the power and control they had over her. Relishing in the connection the three were sharing, Megan committed everything she had to the encounter. Though she'd been on the brink of orgasm several times without being permitted release, she didn't care. As much as Troy and Ransom appeared to be taking, they were giving in equal amounts.

"Good girl," Troy raised from above. "Just another couple of inches, baby."

"Take all of Master, sweetheart," Ransom growled hoarsely, one hand trailing down over her belly and between her spread thighs. "Take every delicious inch of Troy's cock."

Megan moaned around Troy's shaft as Ransom slid a thick finger inside her pussy, struggling to stay as still as she could. Her arousal was getting the better of her as a second finger joined the first, thrusting up into her. The faster her hips gyrated, the harder she pressed back against Ransom, creating exquisite contact with the plug in her ass.

Each time his body jarred the toy, an erotic current pulsed through every nerve ending.

"Do not come," Troy ordered.

Megan craved their dominance. She decided she didn't want to live without it. After experiencing them, she wasn't certain she could.

When the sac beneath Troy's penis touched her chin, Megan thought she would gag. Stroke after titillating stroke, he pushed deeper until she thought she would pass out from carnal overload. Without warning he stopped, and pulled free from her mouth.

Megan sobbed out a protest and reached for him.

"You suck cock very well, slave girl," Troy ground out in a ragged voice.

"T-Thank you, Master," Megan heard herself saying.

"Now turn around and pleasure your fellow slave," Troy told her. "No hands, just your mouth."

Ransom's grip on her relaxed and she turned around in his arms. The sexy grin he flashed her made her lower belly spasm in need. Assuming the doggy style position, Megan waited for his direction.

Staying seated on his heels, thighs open, Ransom wrapped his hand around the back of her neck, urging her face toward his groin.

Once again, Megan found herself only too happy to oblige the man before her.

"Nice and slow, sweetheart," Ransom said.

"Keep that ass high in the air, baby," Troy's voice called in the distance. "It's time to change the plug."

A guttural groan came from above and Ransom's throaty chuckle made her grin.

"She likes the sound of that, Master."

* * * *

As Troy approached his lovers, the sight of Megan's head bobbing up and down between Ransom's thighs had his balls near ready to explode.

The entire time, Ransom held Troy's gaze.

The final thread of Troy's control was tested as he knelt on the flood behind Megan. Her ass, high in the air, round, firm, had his skin tingling. The base of the butt plug nestled between the pale cheeks taunted him to pull it free and replace it with his cock.

Troy groaned, reaching for the toy. His right hand caressed the pale globes of Megan's ass as his left gave a gentle tug on the plug.

"Relax, baby. Let it go," he said.

The sight of her muscles stretching to allow the toy to slip out made his mouth water.

To test her readiness, Troy lubed a couple of fingers and pushed them inside her ass.

"Oh yeah," Ransom growled low. "Our baby likes that, Master. Your thick fingers stroking inside her ass makes her suck my cock harder. That's it, swallow me down."

Feeling his control slipping, Troy wasted no time in prepping the new plug and positioning it. If he didn't get the toy in place and soon, he'd ram his cock inside before Megan was ready to accept him.

The last thing he wanted to do was cause her unnecessary pain.

"Here it comes, baby," Troy said, and slipped the rounded tip past the outer ring of muscles. "Relax."

The toy had been inserted half way when Megan tensed.

Ransom's fingers fisted in her curls, and his right hand reached under to massage her left breast. "Keep breathing, baby," he encouraged. "Relax and push out."

Troy's balls threatened to unload as he watched her hole pulse and flare. He heard Megan struggle for breath, and continued to slide the plug into place.

"Christ," he croaked. "Ah fuck. Just a little more."

Megan gasped around Ransom's cock. She pushed back, opening her rectum to accept the last half inch.

"Jesus, I don't know how long I can hold off before giving in to the need to shove my dick up inside you," he said.

Around the base, Troy watched her muscles throb. After a moment, he caught himself stroking his cock. Control, he reminded himself.

"Easy, Master," Ransom said, his eyes darting between Megan's ass and Troy's hand working over his shaft.

Needing to taste her pussy for himself, Troy spread Megan wider and dipped his head. Feeling like a pubescent school boy, Troy dove in, drilling his tongue as deeply as he could.

The heavy fragrance of Megan's arousal swirled under his nostrils, making his head spin. Now after sampling Megan on his tongue, he could die a happy man.

Regaining some control, Troy withdrew to take a few moments to visually enjoy the beautiful sight before him. The pink petals of Megan's intimate flesh fluttered, and Troy grew entranced as he studied her most private area. The smooth folds glistened with her essence and his urgency.

Again he slipped his tongue inside. His thumb pressed against her pulsing clit as his mouth continued to feast upon her.

As Megan's need climbed, her muffled cries echoed around the room. Pulling back, Troy wiggled the plug with a finger from his left hand, and slid two digits from his right into her pussy.

Wet, snug muscles gripped his fingers, clenching and releasing in time to his thrusting.

"No coming," Troy reminded her with a strangled voice, trying to keep himself in check.

Megan sobbed a protest around Ransom's cock a second before he pulled her head away from his shaft. "Jesus," he gasped, fighting to draw air into his lungs.

Troy caught the strained expression marring Ransom's face, and suspected he'd pulled free with nary a moment to spare.

Having spent the past five years with Ransom as lovers, Troy knew the man had stamina. Ransom could stave off his climax for a couple of hours when they played. Yet after shoving his own cock down Megan's throat, feeling the exquisite sensations her sweet mouth could create, Troy was amazed Ransom held off as long as he did.

Troy realized his efforts to maintain control were weakening by the minute. He needed to bury himself deep inside Megan, and very soon.

Wasting no time, Troy pulled Megan upright, and against him, lowering her to the floor. Meeting Ransom's heated gaze, Troy nodded. Ransom shifted onto his knees and covered Megan's body with his own. Without a word he thrust his hips forward, burying himself balls deep inside her.

"Ah fuck," he growled, and for a moment, stilled.

On either side of Ransom's slender hips, Megan's knees fell open as he pulled back and commenced a furious rhythm.

"Fuck, she's tight, wet, hot," Ransom rasped out.

Troy reached out, cupping Megan's bouncing breasts, squeezing, reshaping, massaging the supple flesh, savoring the vision of Ransom's cock disappearing and reappearing from the depths of Megan's voluptuous, sexy body.

"Tell me how hot her cunt is," Troy said, and Megan whimpered.

"My dick is surrounded by fire. Hot molten lava squeezing me."

Troy dipped his head, sucking the air from Megan's lungs as his lips crushed against hers.

Her hand wrapped around his neck holding him to her, and for a moment he allowed her the control. As the pressure of her hand grew more insistent, with reluctance he pulled away.

"Feel good, baby?" he asked, his finger tips tugging roughly on her distended rosy tipped nipples.

From side to side her head flopped, mewling whimpers of need slipped past her lips. Guttural grunts of passion reverberated from deep in Megan's chest. Heavy perspiration coated her flesh, and in an instant she gasped, struggling for air.

"P-p-please," she cried out.

"What do you need, baby?" Ransom said, through gritted teeth. His own pleasure threatened to push him over the cliff, straining his voice.

"S-st-" she choked out through a sob.

"Say the words," Troy said. "We need to hear the words."

"M-my s-safe w-word?"

Immediately Ransom stopped thrusting, and Troy ceased plucking at her nipples.

Ransom stared down at her, and when she finally opened her eyes, tears filled them. "Sweetheart?"

"Do you want to use your safe word?" Troy asked.

Jesus, things seems to be going so well. What the fuck had they done wrong?

Troy and Ransom exchanged a concerned glance. Beneath Ransom's weight, her body shook violently, as if she were freezing cold.

Megan shook her head. "N-no. No."

"Then what is it, baby?" Troy asked, and wiped away a falling tear. "Tell us what's wrong."

"I d-didn't want to c-come, a-and dis-appoint y-you both," she stammered, still trying to catch her breath.

As her words registered, both men chuckled, and Ransom dropped a kiss on her forehead. "Sweetheart, it's all right."

Troy stroked his fingers through her hair as silence settled between them. Ransom dipped his head several times, sipping at the odd tear that trickled from the corner of her eyes.

After a few minutes Megan appeared a little more composed. A couple moments later, she was able to speak. "I didn't want to come and disappoint you," she repeated.

Troy brushed the back of his finger along her flushed cheek. "Baby, we could never be disappointed in you."

A glint of uncertainty flickered in her eye.

Her reaction bothered Troy. After giving herself so freely to him and Ransom sexually, he wondered why his words caused her doubt.

Megan blew out an exasperated breath. "I don't think I understand how the safe word is supposed to work," she confessed.

"Is that was this is all about?" Troy asked.

"I don't want to use my safe word, but I didn't know what else to do. I really needed a minute," she whimpered, and another tear slipped free. "I was so close to coming, and you kept saying I couldn't."

"It's all right, baby," Ransom assured her. "Honestly. Please stop crying. I'm sorry, I thought you understood earlier, but it's okay. We'll clear things up now. You would use your safe word if one of us did something that didn't feel good for you. Something that hurt, or brought you unbearable discomfort," Ransom said. "Or if we did or suggested something that makes you uncomfortable."

"A little pain, pressure or discomfort is okay, baby. But if something ever hurts, you must tell us," Troy added. "Sex and our playtime together should never hurt."

"But how about like now, when you tell me not to come, and I'm so fucking close I can taste it?"

Troy laughed out, and then kissed her soundly. As he withdrew, desire again simmered in her eyes. His shaft jerked against his thigh, wanting its turn inside her body. First, Megan needed to be assured her consideration was paramount.

"If I tell you not to come it's because I want to prolong the pleasure for all of us. Rest assured I will always allow you to come, but on my terms. When you feel stretched beyond your limit, and you haven't been given permission, then it's okay to say something. Just be sure you are as far as you can go, baby, because if you start yanking my chain, I'll paddle that sweet little behind of yours."

Her eyes danced with interest. Perhaps next time he'd introduce her to a flogging. The thought had the tip of his cock leaking.

Ransom pushed his hips forward, finding Megan off guard, and she gasped.

"Can we get back to playing? I think you've bought yourself enough cool down time," he said.

"I think it's time to reward my two slaves. Lie down," Troy commanded Ransom, and he complied. "Now, climb up and slide your cunt down on his cock." Troy sat back on his heels, watching as Megan did as he asked.

Grabbing the tube of lubricant lying on the floor beside him, Troy squeezed a generous amount into the palm of his hand. As Ransom's shaft disappeared into Megan's body, Troy wrapped his fingers around his length, and stroked long and hard.

"That's it, baby, ride him," Troy said.

On his knees Troy crawled toward his lovers, and settled himself between Ransom's splayed thighs.

Reaching out he grabbed the base of the butt plug, and slowly eased it from Megan's body. Not giving her body a moment to adjust to the emptiness, Troy pushed forward, slipping the broad crown of his dick inside.

Knowing a cock felt different from a butt plug or a dildo, Troy wasn't surprised Megan's ass tensed at the new intrusion.

With his hands, he caressed the pale cheeks he was buried between. When Megan pushed back against the pressure, Troy advanced a couple more inches.

"Jesus, baby. You should see your body taking me in. Your ass is flared out around my cock. Tight and pulsing," Troy said.

From beneath Megan, Ransom's hips pumped upward, driving him deep. Within the snug, warm confines of their lover's body, the stimulation of their firm flesh brushing along one another sparked a barrage of new sensations.

Troy was instantly lost in the feel of Megan's body. In an instant he was snapped back to reality as her ass began to convulse around him, and her body stilled.

"Megan?" he hoped his tone carried the warning intended.

"I-I d-didn't," she sobbed. "But, I-I'm so c-close."

"A little longer, baby. Hold it for us a little longer," he told her.

Troy met Ransom's strained gaze, need dancing in his eyes. They shared a mutual nod, and a moment later Troy gave the final order of that session.

"Now, baby," he growled hoarsely. "Come for us now."

A keening cry burst from Megan's lips, and her body trembled.

Rivulets of sweat trickled all over her flesh.

Ransom's triumphant call immediately followed Megan's, his own body keeping time with her convulsive tremors.

Troy's had never felt anything as amazing as Megan's body around his cock, milking him dry. Her muscled gripped and pulsed with such ferocity Troy thought she may snap him in two.

Megan's climax seemed to strengthen, dragging on, demanding his release. Once affirming his lovers were satisfied, Troy then allowed himself his own release.

As his body unloaded, he lost feeling in his legs, and he swore he blacked out for several seconds. His cocked seemed to jerk on and on inside Megan's velvety snug ass.

Troy had no idea how much time passed, but the sound of Ransom's voice calling to him, had the clouds fogging his mind dissipating.

"Troy? Babe, you okay?"

Realizing he'd collapsed on top of Megan, Troy raised himself on unsteady arms, and gently eased his spent shaft from her backside.

"I think," he stopped and gave his head a shake. "I think I blacked out, Rans."

"I know I did," his lover replied with a chuckle.

"Meg," Troy said, now concerned that Megan hadn't moved once he lifted his weight off her.

Reaching for her at the same moment, Ransom rolled over, easing her to floor, Troy's heart jumped into his throat. He'd hurt her. By losing control, he'd crushed her smaller frame between his and Ransom's bodies.

"Meg," he repeated, cupping her face in his hands.

"She's out, Troy. But she's okay," Ransom said, and stroked a finger down her cheek. "Give her a minute or two, she'll be right back." He stood up and gave a stretch. "I'll go grab a cold cloth for Megan. Be right back."

Troy dipped his head, pressing a kiss to her lips.

"Come on, sweetheart, you're worrying me. I've never had anyone pass out on me before," he told her quietly.

"That's because you weren't with the right woman," she whispered.

Troy chuckled as Ransom knelt beside them. He rubbed a cool cloth over Megan's face and neck, grinning.

"You got that right, sweetheart," Ransom said.

"Can we do that again?" Megan asked, her voice hoarse.

Both men laughed.

"Oh yeah, baby," Troy said. "We're going to do it again."

CHAPTER 4

Following an adult shower the trio snuggled together on a king size bed in Troy and Ransom's room. Megan lay on her back, sated beyond her wildest dreams, knowing a stupid grin curled her lips. On either side of her, stunning men lay. She'd never imagined one could be so relaxed, and yet wired at the same time. Megan was thankful that she'd not encountered such an experience before now, or else she may not have had the opportunity to meet Troy and Ransom.

"You know, I've got to admit that was by far the best orgasm I've ever had," Ransom said, stroking the tip of one finger over the crest of her right breast. "How 'bout you, baby? Feel good?"

"No one has ever brought me to climax before," she confessed freely.

"Are you serious?" he asked.

She nodded. "I have very little sexual experience," she added. "But, that was beyond fabulous. I actually lost the feeling in my limbs. Is that normal?"

Both men chuckled, making her snicker. "That was dumb, huh?"

she asked, relishing the feel of Troy's palm resting possessively on her abdomen.

"Not at all," Troy said.

"Have the two of you been lovers a long time?" she asked, wondering if she was getting too personal. While she was blindfolded, the sounds of Troy and Ransom sharing kisses had sent her pulse racing. As she lay nestled between them, she desired to see them love one another.

Maybe this encounter was simply a night of no-strings-sex for them, and in the morning, if not sooner, she'd be sent on her way. The thought of Ransom and Troy dismissing her had her heart dropping.

"Five years," Troy replied. "We were each other's first male relationship, and it's worked out well for us."

Did they have no room in their lives for another? What would the possibility be of them wanting to see where this experience may take the three of them?

"You seem very in tune with one another," she noted, and a question continued to needle her. "Do you, uh, share women, often?"

Ransom shook his head. "This is a first for us."

"Well you work together like a well oiled machine," she told them. "I know it's not my place to ask—" Megan stopped herself from posing her question. Though she knew very little about the lifestyle, she was certain a sub would never be permitted to question a Master.

"Never be afraid to ask us anything, or to speak what's on your mind, Meg," Troy said. "I mean it. We are equals."

"But you're a Master, how can we be equals?"

* * * *

Troy lowered his lips, and suckled the tip of her left breast thoroughly before answering. "I enjoy dominating my partners in sexual play only. I want to see how far my lovers can be pushed before their world splinters apart as they explode in climax."

He delighted in the shuddering of her body as she digested his statement.

"In all other aspects of life, we are equals."

"You treated me with such respect and consideration when we played. It was sort of like you were caring for me while taking what you wanted," she said, and then stopped to gather her thoughts.

"Yes," Ransom replied. "That's how we enjoy playing."

Troy watched her brow furrow as she considered Ransom's words.

"But I've heard and read that BDSM play can include name calling, and… Well, to be honest, actions that are just plain cruel to the submissive person."

"I have no need or desire to degrade or humiliate my lovers to make me feel good. I've always been a firm believer of anything going on between consenting adults is perfectly acceptable."

"Oh."

"There was a time years ago that I trained potential Doms in the lifestyle, but after—" Troy paused. Megan's introduction in the world so far had been incredibly pleasurable. She didn't need to know about the darker side right now. Though a part of him wanted her to use caution, and be aware of what was out there for those who craved it.

"After a rather unpleasant encounter, Troy gave up training, and focused on what he enjoyed in the lifestyle," Ransom added.

Concern for him filled Megan's brown eyes. "Someone hurt you?"

Troy shook his head. "Not in the physical sense. New clients, a man and woman arrived at my door for a session. I still don't have any idea how they came across me."

Troy glossed over the details as he shared with Megan the experience that changed him.

We ain't new to this, the man sneered as he'd walked into the playroom. In silence Troy recalled the man's words and tone of voice, and a jolt of anger speared him. My old lady just wants someone to watch. Our friends won't anymore. That information should have had Troy thinking twice.

At first, Troy thought he'd be in for quite a show. Despite the man's gruff exterior, he was certain their performance would be a genuine coupling. Something he'd get off on later as he recalled them.

The minute the man ordered the woman to undress, Troy detected something very wrong in his voice. After roughly tying the woman to a bench, Troy spied her hands and feet turning color from the lack of circulation. When he demanded the man loosen the bindings the man snarled, and nearly turned on him.

"The look on the woman's face wasn't one of fear," Troy said, recalling the woman's expression as vividly as if she were standing right in front of him. "Oh no, this experience wasn't one that was new to her. She looked defeated, beaten down."

In silence, she'd allowed her partner to do as he wished. Troy watched as the man withdrew a bullwhip from the duffle he'd brought with him. What happened next occurred so fast that at the time, Troy thought he'd been dreaming.

Over his head the man wielded the whip, bringing it down to strike the intimate flesh between the woman's splayed legs. The piercing scream she gave angered the man, and he leapt on top of her, delivering a single blow to her jaw, rendering her unconscious.

"Without a second thought, I reacted," Troy admitted, blowing out a sigh. "I took the son of a bitch to the ground, and with one shot, knocked him out cold. Once the police and paramedics left my home with the man in handcuffs and the unconscious woman on a stretcher, my life in the BDSM world changed."

Those days were long behind him.

"That woman was very lucky to have crossed your path, Troy," Megan said, cupping the side of his face in her hand. "You know that, right? God, to think of what could have been otherwise."

Megan shuddered.

After that day, Troy had lost many nights' sleep, agonizing over what could have happened.

"It's my desire to assist my lovers in recognizing their sexual limits, and to push themselves past them," Troy told her. "That's what the lifestyle means to me."

Megan seemed to consider what Troy had told her.

"You see, sweetheart, between responsible and consenting adults, anything goes," Ransom said. "But only if all parties are willing. That's why a safe word is important."

"Didn't the woman you were just talking about have a safe word?"

"With a man like the one she was with, a safe word wouldn't have mattered," Troy told her. "The man was into an abuse which had nothing to do with the lifestyle. He had no interest in his partner's pleasure, or any concern for her safety."

"That is so sad," Megan said.

"Is it a very special gift a person can give another when they offer their complete trust regarding their sexual desires," Troy added. "And that gift should be treasured by the person given it."

A few moments passed before Megan spoke.

"All right," she said. "I think I understand. Some people like to control, and others prefer to be controlled. Seems simple enough."

"For some," Troy said.

"Well, I like to be controlled," she admitted. "By the two of you."

"And you're a natural," Ransom told her. "But for others, the decision to submit is one which requires considerable consideration."

"But you are submissive," she said, looking up at him.

"Yes, some of the time," Ransom agreed with a nod. "Well, all right, most of the time. But don't let my submissive nature fool you, baby. I can give just as well as I can take."

"When you're permitted," Troy teased. "Now what did you want to ask us?"

Megan's eyes began to dance, the color darkening as desire again sparked within her.

"I want to see you kiss," she said, her voice taking on a husky tone. "Each other."

Without words, Troy leaned across Megan, Ransom meeting him halfway. Their lips began a tentative exploration of pressure and restrained urgency before their tongues met.

A soft feminine moan sounded between, as they took their time tasting one another.

Megan brushed the softness of her lips against the crook of Troy's neck, bringing his body to immediate attention. He felt the loss of her touch as she pulled away, but the sound of lips kissing Ransom's flesh sent his pulse racing.

The harshness of her breath so near his ear had Troy turning toward her, capturing Megan's mouth with his. His tongue delved inside her sweet mouth, exploring, tasting. The sharp points of her fingernails dug into his forearm, shooting prickles through his body.

With reluctance, Troy pulled back allowing Ransom an opportunity to enjoy her.

"What else would you like to see, baby?" Troy asked, plucking a ripe nipple between his teeth.

Megan looked over at him dreamily, her eyes full of promise, curiosity, and trust.

* * * *

"Show me how you love each other," she heard herself say, surprised to hear the request leave her lips.

The look in both Troy and Ransom's eyes was one of desire, fiery need, and intent.

With the cunning grace of a predator, Ransom crawled over Megan pressing a possessive kiss on her lips, to then pin Troy against the mattress, their mouths meeting hungrily.

The musk of testosterone ignited Megan's arousal as Ransom nibbled a path along the definition of Troy's jaw line. When his tongue flicked out to lick along the pulse of Troy's throat, Megan's fingers stroked down her neck.

Lower Ransom ventured, leaving a trail of moisture as he tasted Troy's tight dark nipples, and down the ripples of a scrumptious six pack.

Glancing up, she spied Troy watching her with intent. Fire blazed in the depth of his gray eyes, and his chest heaved.

"May I kiss you," she asked, needing physical contact with him.

"Yes," Troy replied, but didn't move into her.

Confusion had her replaying his answer.

"Come to me," he commanded.

Megan readily complied. Rising to her knees, she moved in slow, gauging his reaction. His expression never faltered, but his eyes gave away his need.

Close enough, Megan slipped out her tongue, running it over his lips before sliding inside. A sensual sound from Ransom pulled her attention from the oral embrace with Troy.

Glancing down, Megan watched with wide-eyed interest as Ransom's lips closed around the head of Troy's shaft. Slowly, Troy's entire length disappeared.

"Oh God," she groaned, wanting to join Ransom in pleasuring Troy.

"You've felt his mouth on you. You know how good it feels, baby."

"Yes," she whispered.

Megan rested her head on Troy's chest, attention focused on Ransom sucking his cock. Harder her heart pounded against her ribcage. The longer she watched the harder she struggled to breath.

"I'm close, baby," Troy said against the top of her head. "This is what you asked for, so how would you like it to end? Do you want me to come in Ransom's mouth?"

Megan sat up and shook her head. "No," she replied. "I want you to come in mine."

"Come here, sweetheart," Ransom said, glancing up at the two of them.

Megan turned to crawl toward the foot of the bed, but Troy stopped her.

"I'm going to eat your pussy while you suck me off, baby," he said. After settling himself in a semi upright position against the pillows resting against the headboard, he reached for her hips. "Stand up and bend over in front of me," he told her.

Megan's cheeks caught fire, yet she did what Troy asked.

He held her hand as she rose to her feet on the mattress, and stepped one foot over his torso, leaving her backside to his face.

"Bend over. Let me see how wet your pussy is at the idea of swallowing me."

Glancing down, Megan saw Ransom stroking Troy's length in one hand, and his own in the other. "Come down here, baby," he said, holding Troy's shaft in offering.

At the waist Megan bent, leaving her ass high in the air. Troy's hands grabbed her hips firmly, holding her in place. The slide of his tongue along her exposed opening threatened to buckle her knees.

The head of his shaft bobbed before her, and Megan licked her lips before closing her mouth around him.

The combined sensations of giving and receiving had Megan teetering on the edge of climax within minutes.

Ransom's voice said the words she needed to hear. "Baby, you can come whenever you're ready this time."

She whimpered as she came against Troy's tongue. A moment later, Troy's release filled her mouth. The angle her head was at made it tough to swallow, but Megan gave it her all.

Before she had a chance to catch her breath, Ransom's cock brushed against her cheek. Turning her head, Megan barely had time to open her mouth to draw breath before he pushed himself inside.

Troy's hands still gripped her hips, and his tongue and mouth continued feasting upon her pussy.

Ransom placed his hand on the back of Megan's head, holding her in place while he fucked her mouth.

A few moments later he growled low. "Fuck, baby, here it comes."

When she released Ransom's cock Troy eased her hips down, and turned her body so she again lay between them.

"Rest, baby," Troy told her. "We'll be going back into the playroom."

* * * *

As Megan drifted off between them, Ransom watched as Troy's fingers threaded through her tousled blond tresses. The expression on his lover's face was similar to the one Troy looked at him with. Respect, consideration, desire, and love. Ransom also recognized what he himself was experiencing. Protectiveness.

The woman lying between them was theirs. She'd been delivered to them in the same manner they'd been brought to her. Each one of them had something to gain from another.

"The feeling is mutual," Ransom said quietly so as not to disturb Megan.

Troy's lips curled on one side, and despite the dim lighting flickering from the glowing candles throughout their bedroom, Ransom spied him blushing.

"It's that obvious, huh?"

"I just know you, babe." He returned his lover's grin. "I don't want this to end."

"It doesn't have to."

That was true, it didn't have to. "You are a very persuasive man when you set your mind to something."

Troy glanced up, his eyes aflame with need, desire, and want. "Nature has already taken its course. Megan is now aware of what had been missing from her life. It is now our responsibility to show her she's making the right decision in staying with us."

Ransom's brow furrowed and the flesh between his legs began to stir. As he stared into his lover's eyes, and then down at the woman he wanted them to spend the rest of their lives with, he wondered. Could it be as easy as that?

"You seem more confident than usual," he said.

Troy lifted his left shoulder in a half-assed shrug.

"That Megan will remain here, with us," Ransom added. He tamped down his excitement. He wanted nothing more than for her to stay. Hell, it had been a very long time since he'd felt so utterly complete, if he'd ever felt that way at all, and he owed it all to Megan.

Was it possible for them, all three of them, to have found fulfillment in one night? Megan had to feel the same electricity he and Troy were feeling. Didn't she? Ransom wasn't certain his heart would take it if she chose to walk away. The chemistry they shared couldn't be denied.

"A submissive chooses her Master, my love, not the other way around," Troy said, and pressed his lips against Megan's forehead. Her hand weakly swatted at it as if his contact interrupted her sleep, and Troy chuckled. "Our task now is to show our woman she has chosen wisely."

CHAPTER 5

Megan felt herself roused from slumber by erotic sensations stimulating each and every cell in her body. The wet, warm heat of two mouths suckled, nipped and licked at her breasts. The heavy, possessive weight of masculine legs held her thighs apart. Thick fingers thrust a carnal, mind bending rhythm inside her pussy. Two different hands fisted in her curls, holding her head still using acutely different pressures.

She couldn't have moved if her life depended on it. Nor did she have any inclination to do so. When they were finished ravishing her, they would tell her. There was something about knowing her place, where she fit in with them, that brought Megan a sense of purpose. She was so lost in the exotic sensations ricocheting under her skin, Megan couldn't find her voice. A moment later she became fully conscious, and her body exploded, splintering into a zillion fragments of sexual release.

As she lay struggling to catch a breath, Troy's lips crushed against her, stealing what little air she had from her lungs. Only when her fingers dug into his shoulder did he pull back a fraction. His lips continued to brush against hers as he growled, "Playroom. Now."

Their weights lifted off her and Megan's flesh felt chilled. Just as she was about to protest and beg the two of them to take her right there, she recognized Troy's tone of voice had changed. The Dom had stepped forth, and was now calling the shots.

Immediately she caught the gleam of arousal flickering in Ransom's eyes before she lowered her gaze. Without a word she rose up off the bed and followed Troy toward the heavy double doors leading the playroom.

Directing her to stand in the middle of the spacious room, Troy and Ransom spilt off in two different directions. Megan kept her eyes focused on the ground, sensing them moving about.

Troy approached and stood in front of her. Megan watched him reach for her to drag the backs of his fingers from her public bone up to the underside of her left breast. Cupping the soft globe in the warm palm of his large hand, the pad of his thumb brushed across the distended tip. Megan arched her back, pressing her breast into his touch.

From behind, the prickled matting of Ransom's chest hairs tickled against her back.

"Arms up." His hot breath caressed over her shoulder and neck.

Megan did.

Troy stood in front of her, the thick pads of his fingers now plucking at the tight peak of her right breast.

A guttural moan worked its way from deep within her chest, and her body shivered.

Above her, Ransom grasped her small hands in his. The touch of soft leather being wrapped around her writs made Megan lift her head to look up at Troy. Only for a moment, she allowed herself to gaze into his stormy gray eyes before she lowered her head.

Again she groaned as his attentions went back to teasing her left nipple.

"Give a tug, slave girl," Ransom said, licking her earlobe with the wet tip of his tongue.

Megan did as asked, only to find he'd left no slack in the bindings.

"Excellent," he purred, sliding his hands over her hips to cup the cheeks of her ass. "Now spread your legs a little. Just until you feel tension in your arms."

As she slid her feet apart, her body shifted, and Megan emitted a soft moan at the sudden stretching sensation coursing through her limbs.

"Look at me," Troy ordered.

Craving the tone of her Master, Megan's body eagerly met his command.

Full sensual lips were drawn tight, his expression all business, yet his eyes betrayed him. Full of lust, desire, possessiveness, he studied her. To Megan, Troy seemed to be tempering his restraint. How could he be so close to the edge when he was the one in control of the entire experience?

Reading her thoughts, Ransom leaned closer and whispered in her ear. The look of need in Troy's eyes told her Ransom was enjoying their visual exchange. "You test Master, slave girl," he said. "Your sensual femininity. Your innocence," he moaned, and pushed two fingers inside her pussy. "Your eagerness to submit to Master's wants. You are looking at a Master on the edge, slave girl. I hope Master takes mercy on you."

"I don't," she heard herself respond. "Please, Master."

Troy cocked his head, his fingers tugging roughly on her now very sensitive, erect nipples. "Please what, slave girl?"

"Please, Master. Make me yours."

Troy's deep chuckle reverberated through Megan, sending shock waves of lust coursing through her. "You were mine the moment you set foot in my domain, slave girl."

"Yes, Master."

Yours, Megan sobbed inwardly. Beneath their combined touch she was found and lost. Fulfilled, yet so incomplete. All yours.

"Now, since you've been a good girl, I have a gift for you, our slave," Troy announced, and held a pair of dangling jewels for Megan to see. "I purchased these just for you."

Though the item she looked at somewhat resembled a clip on

earring, Megan knew that wasn't what it was.

"They're gorgeous, Master," she said. They sparkled as Troy twirled them between two fingers. His eyes continued to hold hers. "What are they?"

"Clamps for your pretty nipples," he declared, releasing the twin gemstones. Between his fingers he held a fine chain connecting the two clamps.

Megan gasped and began struggling against the binding around her wrists. Christ, his rough attentions, though stimulating and erotic, had made her nipples sensitive. The thought of him attaching those tight, unforgiving looking clips to her tender peaks had her whimpering.

"Now, there's going to be a slight sting as I clamp your pretty nipples." His firm tone warned her to stop struggling. "But I promise intense pleasure will replace it. Breasts as beautiful as yours, slave girl, should be decorated."

Ransom's thick pleasuring fingers continued to probe her, as Troy brought the first clamp toward her left breast. Megan sucked in a breath as Troy released the end, and the rubber tip tightened on her nub.

The metal sparkled and the gem danced in the flickering candle light. As the cool chain brushed along her quivering belly, Megan gasped at the contact.

Once the second clamp was placed, Ransom withdrew his fingers from her body. Her pussy felt so empty, so neglected, and her nipples stung.

Troy grinned, examining his work. "I was correct," he stated, and took the dangling length of chain in his hand. "Look at how beautiful your nipples are adorned with pretty stones."

Megan glanced down at herself as Troy gave an experimental tug on the link of chain. Prickles of pain radiated inward from the tips of her nipples, and her lower belly clenched. Her lower lip dropped as if she were about to speak, but no sound could be heard.

Again he jerked the chain. This time Megan cried out, and moisture flooded her sex. Her nipples felt as though they were on fire, and her entire body warming. The effort it took to draw breath due to the onslaught of carnal sensations made Megan light headed.

"Now I want to watch you whip her, slave," Troy commanded and released the chain he'd been holding.

That did it! Megan was about to pass out.

"Yes, Master," Ransom growled, and released his hold on her.

* * * *

With wide eyed apprehension, Megan stared up at him. Troy read a flash of uncertainty, so brief he wasn't sure he'd seen it. But he had. In less than a heartbeat, intrigue, curiosity and trust settled on her expression. Trust is what he searched for. Though perhaps nervous at the new game, Megan trusted Troy and Ransom to see to her pleasure, and more importantly her safety. And they wouldn't let her down on either account.

The sight of Megan helpless and at their mercy bound to a suspension bar, legs parted, clamps dangling from her nipples, had drops of pre-cum dripping from the end of his cock. His own nipples ached as they tightened and distended.

I am in control, he growled to his betraying body.

Like hell, his dick laughed back.

There was no way in hell he was ever going to let the woman in front of him go.

Behind her Ransom appeared holding his favorite flogger in his right hand. Strips of black leather dangled from a polished stainless steel handle.

Troy recognized the glint of need and lust, desire and determination in his lover's expression, reflecting his own.

"Begin," Troy ordered, and Ransom's arm rose.

When the first strike of the leather straps connected with the pale flesh of her ass, Megan drew up on her toes and her eyes squeezed shut. A few seconds passed before she opened her eyes and looked at him.

"That didn't hurt," she said. "Well, not really."

"It wasn't supposed to hurt," he replied.

Without being directed, Ransom wielded the flogger again, and this time a groan caught in Megan's throat.

"Again," she whispered, and wiggled her ass.

Troy nearly shot his load right then and there.

When Ransom failed to strike her again, she opened her eyes, questioning without words.

A half nod of his head had Ransom swinging again.

Troy reached over and gripped the chain linking the clamps on her nipples between his thumb and forefinger, and tugged sharply.

Megan gasped and sunk her teeth into her lower lip.

"I call the shots," he reminded her.

"Yes, Master," she replied, and dropped her gaze to the weeping flesh sticking straight out from between his legs.

Several minutes passed as Ransom continued to use the flogger against Megan's ass and thighs. Louder her cries grew with each strike of the supple leather straps.

"Paddle," Troy said, his voice having grown hoarse.

"Yes, Master." Ransom's deep voice was laced with enthusiasm.

Ransom turned and walked away, only to return with a thick wooden paddle in hand.

The first crack of the paddle against Megan's left ass cheek made her knees visibly weak.

A second swat brought Troy's gaze between her quivering legs to spots of arousal glistening on Megan's thighs.

Again and again, the sound of wood smacking against Megan's ass and thighs bounced off the walls in the playroom.

Troy's balls tightened against his body, and he reached down to give them a sharp tug to stave off his orgasm, and realized his hand was stroking a furious rhythm on his shaft.

Now near dangling from the suspension bar on shaky legs, her body trembling, Megan sobbed, begging for release. Though he didn't tell her she couldn't come, it aroused him further that she awaited his permission.

Heavy sweat covered Ransom's taut flesh. Between his legs his cock so swollen, the end an angry color purple, Troy couldn't believe he hadn't blown his load already. His lover's shaft looked sore.

"Fuck her ass," Troy managed to utter hoarsely out at Ransom, his own climax threatening.

Without a word, Ransom dropped the paddle to the floor and reached for a tube of lubricant from beside his foot. The sound of the gel squishing out of the bottle had Megan moaning.

Troy watched her eyes widen as Ransom used his fingers to stretch her before shoving his cock inside.

Holding Troy's gaze from behind Megan, Ransom's hips pushed forward, and Megan cried out as he slid himself to the hilt.

Ransom's left hand wrapped around Megan, his fingers disappearing between her legs, and his right grasped a hold of the chain, giving a slight tug on the length.

Troy watched, rapt for several moments, and his two lovers moved together. Louder Megan cried as she held on for dear life to the last thread of her control.

"Now," Troy growled.

Needing only that one word, Megan blew apart. As her body became limp, Ransom's hoarse cries of release filled the room.

Troy approached the two, panting heavily struggling for air, and placed a kiss on Megan's damp forehead before dropping one on Ransom's mouth. As he unclipped the clamps from her nipples, she blew out a sigh. Above her he reached to unfasten the buckle around her wrists. Boneless, Megan collapsed against his chest, and with little effort he scooped her up into his arms.

After placing another chaste kiss on Ransom's mouth, Troy turned with Megan in his arms and left the playroom. Across the plush carpeting of the bedroom, he carried Megan, and placed her in the middle of their king size bed.

Without words he leveled himself over her quivering frame, and settled his slender hips between her spayed thighs. As she opened her eyelids and looked up at him, Troy slid his cock into her warm, wet depths, and sighed.

Heaven. He was in heaven. There wasn't a more beautiful, more welcoming place on earth than inside Megan's luscious body.

Beneath him she lay whimpering, mewling as he pushed her spent body higher. Again she would come, and this time her cunt would pulse around him. Milk him.

"Do you have any idea how incredibly sexy you are when you come?" he asked, grunting in between thrusts. "Any idea how fucking gorgeous I think you are at this very moment?" The tips of her fingers dug into his forearms as Troy withdrew and stroked even deeper.

Around his waist Megan's legs wrapped, hooked at the ankles, holding him against her.

The scent of her arousal taunted Troy's senses. The fragrance swirled under his nostrils, and he could taste her on his tongue.

"I can't get enough of you," Troy confessed, and pulled her left nipple between his lips. Releasing it with a pop, he drew the right peak into his mouth.

The bed dipped beside them as Ransom joined them.

Higher off the bed Megan's back arched, pressing her flesh against him. Megan's skin glistened with sweat, and Troy could no longer resist tasting the salty liquid.

He was so close, and needed her to reach orgasm at the same moment he did.

"You feel so fucking good, gripping my dick, Megan. Jesus, woman," he groaned. "You are so close, baby. So fucking close."

* * * *

"Yes, Master," she said.

"No, baby," Troy said, stilling his hips. "You don't have to call me Master when we make love. That is saved only for our time in the playroom."

Confusion creased her brow as she looked between Troy and

Ransom.

"There is a difference, sweetheart," Ransom said, nuzzling her neck. "Think about it. Remember the sensations, the feelings, the emotions you experienced in the playroom?"

Megan replayed the visions of their encounters in the playroom. Inside the walls of the playroom, Troy and Ransom had been rough, demanding, controlling. Their actions and words had been possessive, authoritative, and beyond arousing. Her body responded to their requests and demands willingly, eagerly, with desperate need.

"It was so primal," she said, breathlessly. "Uninhibited. Surreal."

As her mind enjoyed its homemade x-rated movie, Troy commenced a slow, sensual stroking inside her again. Megan moaned, giving into the pull, the need to be loved by him.

"Tell us how this is different, baby?" Troy asked, kissing her with a deliberate and intense oral embrace.

Megan focused on the sensations, and the two men. Now their caresses were gentler, they were attentive, attuned to her needs and desires. Not that they weren't all those wonderful things in the playroom, but now the entire atmosphere encompassing them was...different. It was as if they were loving her. Making love with her.

Making love.

Their claiming was still possessive, and protective, yet unhurried. Troy and Ransom continued to take what they wanted from her body, but not until satisfied with her contentment.

Megan never wanted to be anywhere else.

Ever.

* * * *

It was important to Troy and Ransom, that Megan realize the experience they were sharing was one the two men took seriously. Both had hoped this evening would be the beginning of something beautiful and long term, if not permanent between them.

"Do you have any idea how much you mean to us?" Troy whispered against her lips.

"Please," she whimpered, and thrust her hips to meet his. "Troy," she said, and then looked at Ransom to her left. "Ransom."

"Let go, sweetheart," Ransom said, holding her gaze "We're here to catch you."

"Always," Troy told her. "Always, our baby."

Megan's body tightened around his pounding flesh. Faster Troy thrust, drawing her climax out. Before her clenching muscles subsided, he drove himself deeper, falling over the edge of the cliff.

All around him bright lights popped, glass shattered, as his throbbing testes emptied.

Exhausted, Troy collapsed atop Megan, and her hands caressed soothingly over the tensing muscles in his back and ass.

"That was amazing," Megan sighed.

"I agree." Troy pulled his semi hard shaft from Megan's heat.

Holding her in his arms, he rolled, taking her with him.

Across his broad chest, Megan drifted off to sleep.

Settling himself against her back, Ransom shifted, and pulled a blanket lying at the bottom of the bed up and over the three of them. "I love you," he said, pressing a kiss between Megan's shoulder blades, and then glanced at his lover. "Both of you."

CHAPTER 6

As Megan edged closer to consciousness, the scent of Ransom under her nose conjured up the carnal images of the previous night. With his arms wrapped around her, she realized the experience she shared with Troy and Ransom had changed her. In a matter of hours she'd become a sexually liberated woman.

She couldn't believe how easily the two men played her body. It was as if she'd been made solely for them. The intense pleasure they'd wrung from her more-than-willing and eager body stunned her.

Megan didn't want anything more than to stay with Troy and Ransom. But would that be a possibility in the light of day?

"Good morning, sweetheart," Ransom said, tightening his arms.

Megan sighed, and snuggled in closer to him. "G'morning." Behind her the bed felt empty. That thought made her uneasy. Shifting, she glanced over her left shoulder, and her heart sank. It seemed Troy couldn't wait to put an end to their time together. She wondered how soon after she fell asleep that he bolted. "Where's Troy?" she asked, yet wasn't certain she was prepared for Ransom's answer.

"Making breakfast. We flipped for it earlier, and he lost. Or maybe you and I did. We'll have to see what he comes up with." Ransom chuckled and dropped a kiss on the top of her head. "The man can't cook worth a damn."

"But he's something else in the lovin' department," Megan said, and hoped Ransom caught the sincerity and need in her voice. She didn't care if she sounded desperate, she wanted them, both of them.

"That he is," he said in agreement, holding her close.

Megan needed Ransom and Troy. That was all there was to it. Together, they'd shown her what she was missing in her life. To be dominated was something she never realized she needed to complete her until she'd had a taste of it.

"All right you two," Troy's voice announced his entrance in the bedroom. "It isn't much, but I'm hoping you'll appreciate my efforts." He laughed.

Megan untangled her limbs from Ransom's and they sat upright. Finding herself confused, Megan wondered how in the hell she was going to make them see that with them was where she wanted to be.

Ransom took the serving tray from Troy's hands and placed it in the middle of the bed. The sheet covering them settled around her waist, and she left it there, leaving her breasts on display. Hell, it might work to her advantage.

The mattress dipped as Troy climbed on the bed, and he placed a gentle kiss against her temple.

"Hungry?" he asked.

Megan returned his smile with one she'd hoped was sexy and inviting, and nodded. "Famished."

They took turns feeding her rubbery scrambled eggs and bites of toast that bordered on being burnt. As they ate, Megan continued setting herself up for being hurt. The more she thought of it, and watched Troy and Ransom interact, things became clearer. She realized the two men, lovers, didn't have room in their lives for a clingy little rich girl who...

"Hey, what's made you fall so quiet, baby?" Troy asked, pushing a lock of hair behind her ear. "Breakfast that bad?"

Megan let out a heavy sigh. There was no need in drawing things out. "Breakfast has been a really nice touch, but..."

"But what, sweetheart?" Ransom asked.

"We're just prolonging the inevitable. The end of our experience."

"The end?" Troy asked, and exchanged a glance with Ransom. "Oh, are we finished here?"

"Well—" she began, only to be cut off.

"Troy and I sort of thought this was a beginning," Ransom said, meeting her gaze. "Not an ending."

"This was...sex. Great sex. An unbelievable experience. An eye opener for me," Megan said. "And as much as I want to st—" Dropping her gaze, she reached for a plump strawberry and popped it in her mouth before she said something really stupid, and made a fool of herself. "Never mind."

Tense moments of silence stretched out between the three of them. Then Troy placed his finger under her chin, and lifted her head so she had no choice but to look at him.

"Last night was a first for Ransom and me. We are not in the habit of bringing women up here for the sake of sex, or any other reason, for that matter. Megan, you are the first woman we've wanted to share, and to share ourselves with." The sincerity with which he spoke brought a tear to Megan's eye.

"Oh, Troy," she whispered.

"We're not finished, baby," Ransom said, gaining her attention. "We have no reason to lie to you, or string you along. Troy and I want you to stay with us. Hell, the three of us are an exceptional fit together. We love what we've learned about you in the bedroom, but there's so much more to Megan Washington than that."

They couldn't be serious.

Megan laughed. "What if you guys don't like the dud that I can be out of the sack?"

Troy shrugged. "Then we've always got the sex."

"I'm a shop-aholic. And I never throw my dirty socks in the laundry hamper."

"Whatever." Ransom chuckled. "Neither do I, baby."

"I think I might drool in my sleep."

"So? Ransom farts in his," Troy said.

Ransom shrugged, unconcerned at the off-the-cuff remark.

"And when I'm suffering from PMS I eat ice cream right out of the tub."

"I drink out of the milk carton," Troy said.

"Oh God, you do?" Ransom asked, feigning disgust. "I don't know if I can live with either of you now."

The three of them laughed.

"All kidding aside, Meg," Troy interrupted their playful banter. "Can you see yourself settling with a couple of bi lovers who desire to take care of your every need? Do you think you could be happy with us?"

They were serious.

The tears began to flow, and Megan let them. Never in her life did she want anything more. She could be theirs. They would share her, and she them.

"Do you mean it?"

"Haven't you learned anything from our adventure together? A Master is only as good as his submissive," Troy told her, wiping a tear from her cheek with the pad of his thumb. "Baby, I've lived this lifestyle a long time, and I'm not afraid to admit that you've taught me something too."

"Really?" She sniffled. "What's that?"

"Life is way too short," he said. "While you were snoring away—"

"I don't snore," she balked, narrowing her eyes at him.

On the other side of the bed Ransom laughed. "Oh yes you do, baby, but it's really quite cute," he said before placing a kiss on the tip of her nose when she turned to scowl in his direction.

"You are an ass," she snickered. "Both of you."

"Speaking of asses," he said, slipping his hand beneath her to squeeze the cheek of her backside.

"Knock it off, we're trying to have a serious conversation here," Megan giggled as she chastised. "Sort of."

"Maybe it's time for us to come clean," Troy said. "Baby, we have a confession."

"What's that?"

"Well, last night had been a set up, of sorts," he said.

"Some of it, anyway," Ransom added.

Confusion plagued her, and judging by the looks they gave her, it was evident.

"Last night wasn't Dani's first time at the club, and it was her and Max's idea to set something up with him and Natalie," Troy stated.

"What? Dani's been coming here? I guess that explains her goo-goo eyes with the doorman. What's his name? Mikey?"

"Ahh, it's just Mike." Troy chuckled. "Besides his mother, there's only one other person who gets away with calling him 'Mikey'."

"That wasn't all to last night," Ransom said.

"Dani told us about you, and how she recognized the look of a submissive in your eyes. Don't get me wrong. You exude confidence by the bucketful, but your need to be dominated, sexually anyway, is pretty clear. So, she wanted us to show you what it could be like," Troy said.

The sudden anger and humiliation surging through her, exploded.

"Oh I get it now," she snarled, reaching for the sheet to cover her breasts. "This was just some pity fucking then?"

"No," they answered in unison, their voices raised.

"The minute you caught my eye, I was hooked," Ransom told her. "But the rules in play were you had to come to me—to us. There is no way we would have taken you against your will, Megan. That's not what this is, or was about."

Although his admission brought her some comfort, there was still another body in the bed.

"And what about you? The big bad Dom—"

Troy silenced her by capturing her mouth with his, sucking the air from her lungs. Megan reached for him, needing him closer. Digging her fingertips into the muscles of his biceps brought a ragged groan from the depths of Troy's chest.

When he pulled away she stared back into his eyes, gasping for breath, her entire body on fire for him.

"You've allowed yourself to get caught up in the rumors, baby. Allow me to put that to rest. I like to dominate in my sexual play, and only with my lovers. I don't train people anymore, I told you that, except in a certain instance. I may be an astute business man, a real prick in a meeting, and I'm more than aware of the reputation I have out there. That's a far as my 'big bad Dom persona' goes. I know what I like, and I take what I want. But always remember, taking doesn't come without giving," he said, and then kissed her once again. "Now, back to what we were saying. While you were sleeping, Ransom and I were talking."

"'Bout what?" she asked, attempting to gain composure.

"That we are looking for more in our lives," Ransom said.

Megan shrugged with confusion. "O-kay."

"As a couple, Ransom and I have decided another body in our lives would complete our family," Troy added. "In our type of relationship, it is called a third."

"Oh," Megan replied feeling deflated. What the hell was with them? Building her hopes up, to then shoot her down. Did they have no idea what they were doing to her? "You were thinking about a puppy?"

"No," Ransom told her. "We're not getting a puppy. Well, not unless you want one."

"You're losing me," Megan admitted. God, why were they torturing her?

"Honey," Ransom said, seeming to study her confused expression. "We are going to prove to you, every day if necessary, that we mean every word we say to you. That you can count on every promise we make to you."

"Listen, baby," Troy interrupted, gaining her attention. Tucking a stray lock of her hair behind her left ear, his smile was full of promise. His eyes flickered with desire. "As in love as Ransom and I are with each other, there's a piece missing in each of us."

The room fell quiet. Megan's raspy breath the only sound.

"That piece is you," Ransom said.

Megan sat between Troy and Ransom, speechless. How was it even possible for them to lay their emotions and feelings toward her right out there in the open? They'd just met her. Okay, it didn't matter that she felt the same way, but guys weren't supposed to be so forthright.

"Do you believe in love at first sight?" Troy asked her.

Megan shrugged, noncommittally. "I sup-pose," she answered.

"Well, we do," Ransom continued.

Before Megan could speak, one of the cellphones on the nightstand began to ring.

Ransom reached over and scooped the two of them up. After glancing at the display screen, he handed one to Troy. "It's Mike, from the bar phone downstairs."

Troy narrowed his eyes as he flipped open the cover.

"Hey, Mike."

While Troy conversed with Mike, Ransom leaned over and nuzzled Megan's neck.

"No, no it's all right," Troy said. "What's up?"

"Well, what do you think?" Ransom asked, urging her to lie down.

"That I don't want you to stop," she replied, as he leveled his body over hers.

He chuckled, and looked into her eyes.

"What can Troy and I do to persuade you into moving in here with us?" he asked, lowering his mouth to her exposed right breast.

You're doing a fine job! Megan sighed as his lips closed around her nipple.

"Move in?" Megan groaned in arousal. "Are you guys serious?"

"Mmm hmm," he murmured against her flesh.

"I keep thinking I'm going to wake up, and this will all turn out to be a very pleasant dream," she admitted.

"You're not dreaming, baby," Ransom said, pressing Megan against the mattress.

Ransom slid inside Megan's body just as Troy ended the call. Megan's back arched up off the bed.

Troy leaned over and placed a kiss on her quivering lips. Lower his mouth trailed to her left breast. After laving the tight tip with his tongue, he suckled the nub.

Fire smoldered deep in her belly as Ransom stroked teasingly along the fluttering walls of her pussy. She moaned as his tempo increased. "Yes."

"Not yet, baby," Ransom instructed in a soft voice as she reached for orgasm. "Hold on a little longer for me."

"I'll try," she whimpered.

Megan's body continued to climb toward an explosive climax. She was powerless to stop it.

"Troy," she gasped, as his pressure increased on her nipple. "Ransom, please."

A moment later Ransom consented, and together they met a simultaneous culmination.

"That was beautiful," Troy commented, releasing her breast. "And I'm so sorry, but I'm needed downstairs."

"What's wrong?" Megan asked, and sighed as Ransom slipped from her body.

"It seems the daughter of our State Senator was photographed entering our establishment last night," Troy said as he rose from the bed.

Megan stiffened.

"Big deal. Just as many celebs as common folk walk through our doors," Ransom said.

"True, but this is a first where a father storms in, threatening to take us to task," Troy added, pulling a pair of blue jeans up and over his hips, sans boxers.

"Oh, good God," Megan croaked. "He's here?"

Troy nodded. "'Fraid so, sweetheart. And he's none too happy."

"Interesting," Ransom said and left the bed.

Very interesting, Megan thought. As aggressively as the man had lobbied to prevent the opening of the club, Megan couldn't fathom him taking a single step through the front door.

"To what do we owe the displeasure of his presence?" Ransom asked, as he tugged on his jeans.

"Seems our beauty and her girlfriends made this morning's paper," he replied, smiling at Megan.

"You're sure it's my dad?" she asked in disbelief.

"The very same," Troy replied. Taking a deep breath and slowly exhaling, he studied her a silent moment before adding, "The man whose only use for women is to warm his bed."

Megan gasped. How in the hell did Troy know about her father?

Answering her unasked question, Troy said, "When he was making things difficult for us, I had a contact of mine crawl so far up your father's ass, I found out about his extramarital activities, among other things which I have no intention of sharing with you." His tone left no room for discussion on the matter. "When he first refused to back off, I threatened to go public with the information."

Megan realized she was grinning, yet felt far from happy. "It's funny, all these years he thought no one knew, or would ever find out. He has no use for women except when he can fuck them, or their votes can keep him in office." She folded her hands in her lap and glanced aimlessly around the room. "You know," she muttered. "You guys need a little bit of a feminine touch around here. There's a lot of testosterone in your current decorating."

Both men chuckled low.

Reaching over, Troy stroked the back of his finger across her cheek. "You are more than welcome to add your touch to anything around here, baby. Hell, if you don't think you'll be happy living here, we'll buy you a house. Whatever you want."

"I don't need a house," she replied. "Just need you guys."

A heavy sigh blew past her lips and she leaned into his caress.

"When he was home, there was so much shouting, arguing. The berating, the belittling of my mom and me... I never understood why. It doesn't matter what I ever do, I just never measure up in his eyes." Now totally embarrassed at her confession, Megan dropped her chin to her chest. "I honestly can't remember him ever bothering with my mom or me, unless we were needed for some PR stunt, or to throw stuff at us..."

"Oh baby, I'm so sorry," Ransom told her, lifting her chin with his index finger. "It's his loss."

Megan nodded. "Yeah. I know."

"Why don't you stay up here, sweetheart?" Troy said. "We'll sort things out with your father, and then—"

Megan leapt from the bed and raced across the plush carpeted floor toward the closet. "No way, I'm coming with you." There was no way in hell she was going to allow Troy and Ransom to face her father without her. "You don't know my dad. When he's mad, he's…" Flinging the doors wide, she rifled through the clothes hanging neatly on hangers until she found a t-shirt and a pair of sweat pants. With items in hand, she spun around and held them up. "Do you mind?"

Ransom shrugged and shook his head. "Not at all."

Pulling them on, she finger-combed her hair and glanced back up at her two lovers.

"He's pissed, baby," Troy said. "I heard him cursing a blue streak when I was speaking with Mike. I don't want you anywhere near him right now."

"My dad would never hurt me, Troy. At least I don't think he would." Her tone sounded unconvincing even to her own ears. "Hurting me would actually involve physical contact with me," she said. "But when I've done something that might tarnish his image, he gets really angry—"

* * * *

Troy read the determination on Megan face, and knew this particular battle wasn't his to win. "Fine," he uttered. "But stay close to Ransom or myself. Please," he told her.

"He won't hurt me, Troy. I promise."

With a reluctant nod of his head, Troy took her hand in his, and led them down to the bar of the club.

The raised voice of the Senator carried into the corridor separating the common area of the club and the entrance to the private suites.

"Where is she?" they heard as they walked along the wide hallway.

"Oh Jesus," Megan groaned.

"Yup, sounds like daddy's rather fired up." Ransom chuckled to lighten the mood.

As they opened the door and entered the common area, Megan's grip on his hand tightened.

On either side of the belligerent politician stood four large bodyguards, two on each side, standing at ease.

"Senator, I'm going to have to ask you to lower your voice, please." Troy said, attempting to interrupt the Senator's tirade.

"If you think for one minute that you're going to tell me what to do, young man, you're out of your fucking mind. And you," he snarled, pointing a shaky finger towards Megan. "How dare you sully my reputation in this manner? You selfish, spoiled brat."

"What exactly is it that our Megan has done to 'sully your reputation', sir?" Troy asked, composure intact.

"What the hell were you thinking coming into a place like this?

The reporter who shot this photo," he hollered, holding a newspaper over his head, "said he sat out front for hours, and you didn't come out. Do you know how many reporters are parked out front of this shit hole right now?"

"And?" Troy asked.

"And it sure as shit looks like she spend the night! Look at you! Did you spend all fucking night lying on your back with your God damned legs in the air?"

"That'll be enough of that" Troy snarled. "You will not speak to Megan that way."

Senator Washington shot him a look of contempt, and bared his teeth. "For Crissakes girl, what the hell did you do here all night?"

"That isn't any of your business, Senator," Ransom said in a calm tone.

The Senator turned his gaze of anger toward his daughter. After several moments, his face turned bright red. "You let these two fuck you, didn't you? Do you have any idea how this is going to affect me once this gets out? You're no better than a slut. You're just a common whore."

"Dad," Megan gasped.

"Why you son of a bitch," Ransom exploded, but Megan's hand on his chest stopped him from advancing on her father.

Instead of taking a step forward to protect the Senator, each of the four bodyguards took a step backward.

Megan released Troy's hand and took several steps toward her father. Troy and Ransom stayed close.

"Dad please, calm down—"

"You are a disgrace. A huge disappointment. To think I wasted my sperm creating you."

Megan's body stiffened and the color drained from her face. The hurt in her brown eyes infuriated Troy beyond words.

"Now you get your worthless ass out the back fucking door, and into my limo," Megan's father said through gritted teeth. "We'll join my team doing damage control from home."

The air stood still as if time had stopped. The anger frustration and confusion radiating off Megan tore Troy up inside. Judging by Ransom's body language, he was doing his best to remain calm.

"We meant what we said, honey," Troy said, keeping his eyes on the angry man, berating his and Ransom's woman. "You don't have to go anywhere."

"Your home is right here with us, baby," Ransom added. The possessive tone of voice his lover used matched his own.

Following several tense moments, Megan pulled herself tall, and shook her head. "No Dad. I'm not going anywhere."

"Don't you dare back talk me, you hussy," the Senator snapped, and attempted to hit Megan with the newspaper in his hand.

Troy pulled Megan to him. Without argument, she placed herself behind his body.

With lightening speed, Ransom grabbed the Senator's wrist in mid air.

Again, the bodyguards remained in place.

"Whoa, old man," Ransom growled. The grip he held on the other man's hand had the Senator wincing as he lowered it.

"Are you four baboons going to do something?" Senator Washington snarled over his shoulder.

The man standing on his immediate left lifted his chin. "I don't think so, sir. These fellows have things well in hand."

"You were hired to protect me," the Senator roared. "And I expect you to do your job, asshole. Arrest them. Do something!"

The man stood his ground. "I don't know who the hell you think you are, but I'm not about to offer assistance to a political figure, or any man for that matter, who attempts to hit his daughter, and speaks to her like you just have."

"Why you bastard. You are fired!"

"Since you don't pay my wages, sir, that's not your call," the man replied calmly. "But I'm more than happy to put in for reassignment."

"Now, Senator," Troy said. "You will leave without further incident."

"I'm not going anywhere without my daughter."

The sound of the door to the private corridor opening, combined with soft feminine giggling, drew the attention of the crowd in the bar.

Max Renfrew, the club owner entered with Megan's friend Natalie on his arm. Max wore a pair of silk boxer shorts and nothing else. Natalie's upper body was covered with one of Max's t-shirts.

"I'm sorry. I wasn't expecting anyone to be down yet," Max said, and then took a moment to survey the situation. His eyes narrowed with concern. "What's going on here?"

"Natalie?" Megan said in surprise at seeing her friend.

"Meg?" Natalie replied.

"The Senator was just leaving," Troy informed Max.

"The hell I am."

"Senator Washington!" Natalie gasped, and stepped in behind Max, pulling at the hem of the t-shirt.

"Well, seeing you here does not surprise me," the Senator said. "What the hell have you gotten my daughter into?"

"Now you wait just a minute, sir," Max said, taking a step forward. "Senator, you will leave my establishment now, or I'll be placing a call to the police and filing a harassment suit."

"Max? You... You own this club?" Megan asked.

Max nodded in her direction as the back door opened again, and Dani's voice stopped everyone cold.

"Where's my super hunky slave boy at? Yoohoo, Mikey, baby. Your Mistress wants to plaaayyy."

When she came into view, several startled gasps, and a couple strangled groans were heard.

Dani stood in front of everyone, feet apart, wearing a leather corset with holes in the center of the breast cups and her rosy-tipped nipples completely exposed. The scrap of black leather she was trying to pass off for panties left nothing to the imagination. In her right hand she held the handle of a riding crop.

"What the hell is going on?" she said calmly, yet curious. Her eyes settled on Mike. "I thought you came down here to grab us some water?" she asked.

Looking her up and down wearing a broad grin, Mike shrugged. "Something came up," he said, thumbing toward the group of bodies she seemed to have forgotten about.

"I should have known you and the other tart were behind this," Megan's father said.

"Hey, who are you calling a tart?" Natalie screeched, stepping out from behind Max.

Tipping her head coyly, a sly, knowing grin curled her lips. "Nice to see you here without your usual disguise, Senator," Dani said.

The Senator turned white as a sheet. "Why you smug little trollop!" he growled.

Troy had witnessed enough. Megan's father or not, the man would not be permitted to berate and belittle Megan or her friends for what they'd done.

"This meeting is over," Troy said, turning to Megan. "Sweetheart, you take Natalie and Dani up to our suite. Yours, Ransom and my home."

"Troy," she whispered.

"Our home," he repeated.

Troy used the pad of his thumb to wipe away a single tear trickling down her cheek. "We will see your father and his escorts out, then we will be right up."

Megan nodded, the look of complete trust in her eyes for him, set Troy's body on fire. He would protect her and keep her safe to his dying day if she allowed him.

"I love you, Megan," he said for all to hear. "Now, go."

As she turned to do as he asked, Ransom grabbed her forearms and spun her around to face him. Holding the angry gaze of her father a moment longer, Ransom dropped his mouth to Megan's, kissing her long and hard.

When the Senator took a step toward them, the bodyguard on his right stopped him. "Don't even think about it," the man said.

Ransom pulled away and looked into her face. "I love you too, baby." Urging Megan to the door leading to the private suite, he released her.

Once the door closed indicating the women were gone Troy, Ransom, Mike and Max advanced.

Two of the bodyguards who hadn't said a word were young, very young, and clearly lacking experience, appeared to be sizing up the competition. Troy easily read their deduction.

Of the quartet on the club's side of the altercation, Max was the smallest in stature. Yet despite being clad in a pair of silk boxers, his six-one, two-hundred-fifteen pound presence was threatening. Mike was the largest in height and weight, standing six-five and tipping the scales around two-hundred-seventy-five pounds. Ransom was no slouch at six-three, two-hundred-thirty pounds. And Troy himself, had ten pounds on his lover.

"We are done here, gentlemen," Troy said. "Senator or not, and at this moment I don't give a flying fuck you're Megan's old man, you have ten seconds to get the hell out of this club."

"I'm not leaving my daughter with you two miscreants, in this dump that promotes your dysfunctional way of life."

"Get him out, now," Troy said, the warning heavy in his tone.

"Senator," the man to his right spoke. "Sir, my men and I are leaving…with or without you."

The Senator remained quietly fuming.

"Sir, last warning," the man said again. "Let's go."

"I am not finished with you," the angry politician threatened, pointing at each of them.

"Looking forward to seeing you again, Senator," Troy replied.

* * * *

Back in Ransom and Troy's suite, Megan paced, her mind racing.

What the hell was going on downstairs?

"Sit down, Meg," Dani said. "You're going to wear a path in the carpet."

"Downstairs you said something about my dad," Megan said, coming to a halt and staring at Dani.

Her friend nodded. "I've seen him in the club area a handful of times since I started coming here. He wore the same lame-o disguise, which I could totally see right through. I knew exactly who he was the minute I laid eyes on him." Dani stopped talking and gave Megan a half shrug. "You know, I thought it sort of funny since he was such a prick about stopping this place from opening."

Before Megan could pose another question to her friend, Natalie interrupted.

"Any chance you could cover up your nipples?" Natalie asked.

Dani frowned. "Why? I've got great nipples," she groused, pushing her chest out.

Natalie rolled her eyes.

"So, did you girls have a nice time last night?" Dani asked with a knowing grin.

The door to the suite opened and all four men entered.

"Well?" Megan asked.

"Let's just say I doubt the Senator will be sending the club a Christmas card this year," Ransom said, strolling toward Megan. Once close, he gathered her in his arms, and dropped a kiss on the top of her head. "You okay?"

"I'll be fine. I'm used to his tirades."

"You sure you're all right, Megan?" Max asked as he stepped through the door.

She nodded.

"Okay, well, now that that unpleasantness is concluded, the group of us has reservations at The Cove for brunch. A limo will be here in an hour to pick us up," Max announced, and crossed the room to Natalie.

"That's nice," she said, and accepted his hand rising to her feet. "What's the occasion?"

"We're celebrating the first day of the rest of our lives," Max replied. "Come on, move that sweet ass, Nat. I'd like to make love to you before we leave."

"Ah damn! An hour doesn't give me nearly enough time to punish, my Mikey," Dani said with a sassy grin. "That's all right, we'll do a quickie now, and then a longie when we get back."

"Sounds good to me, babe," Mike said, and picked Dani up, tossing her over his shoulder.

When the three of them were alone, Megan blew out a heavy sigh.

"What is that all about?" Ransom asked.

"Couple'a things. First, I'm thinking about my mom. And second, my being here has created such a mess for you guys. And Max," she said. "Maybe I should just go. If I stay, shit like this with my dad will happen all the time. You guys deserve better."

"If your mom is ready to get out, we'll help her, baby," Ransom told her.

"Your father isn't going to be an issue anymore. For you, or for our family," Troy said. Coming up behind her, he wrapped his arms sandwiching her between him and Ransom.

That sounded so perfect. A family, with Ransom and Troy. In the aftermath of the scenario with her dad, the prospect of a happily-ever-after family seemed just out of her reach.

"Listen," Troy said, placing a kiss on the top of her head. "Everything happens for a reason, sweetheart. We need you. Ransom and I want you. You don't have to go anywhere if you don't want to." After a handful of silent moments passed between the hugging trio before Troy asked, "Do you want to leave, baby?"

Without thought, Megan shook her head. "No. I want to stay right here, with the two of you. My life was so incomplete before I met you. Before we shared last night. Now I can't see my life without you. Either of you. I don't want to. Does that make me sound weak and pathetic?"

"Hardly," Troy assured her, sliding his hand underneath the t-shirt she wore.

The brush of his warm, strong flesh against her belly, holding her with possession made Megan's lips curl. Yes, this is where she was meant to be. Her body caught fire. Her nipples tightened, and her sex began to pulse. She was exactly where she wanted to be. Deliciously squished between Troy and Ransom, feeling loved, protected, and cherished.

Christ! Megan suddenly realized something very important.

"Hey, all this talking is cutting into our hour," she blurted out. "And right now, I want to be ravished by the two of you. In our bed."

"Oh I like the sound of that. Our bed." Ransom bent down and scooped her up in his arms. "I'm certain we can accommodate you."

"Me too," Troy said, following them into the bedroom.

"And then when we come back from brunch," she giggled. "I want to do it again."

"You got it, baby," they said in unison.

Yes, My
Mistress

PROLOGUE

A morning breeze drifted in the open patio door, causing the sheer drapery to move like gentle waves washing against a sandy shoreline. In the soft wind the subtle fragrance of annuals in the planters adorning the balcony carried the scents of springtime into the apartment. The only sound in the kitchenette—the faint wisp of turning pages.

Seated on a barstool with her legs outstretched, ankles crossed, Dani Miller sipped a spicy Chai tea while a half-eaten chocolate chip scone sat abandoned on a plate beside her teacup.

She placed the copy of *In the Know* on the breakfast nook to her right. Her cheeks began to heat. The tingling between her legs sent a chill up her spine. She shivered as her arousal gained in momentum. Her mind conjured up images of the vibrator hiding in the top drawer of the nightstand beside her bed, and moisture pooled at the juncture of her thighs. She giggled into the emptiness of her apartment. That toy was going to make her late for work.

A year earlier the magazine *In the Know* was the only print media to be given an exclusive by Le Club d'Esclavage. They'd dedicated over half the edition to the upcoming opening of the club. Natalie Buchanan, one of Dani's best friends, held the position of copy editor with the magazine, and gave her an advance copy of the edition.

Le Club d'Esclavage had been the newest sensation to hit their city. Roughly translated as "The Club of Slavery," it turned the entire community on its ear when its grand opening attracted record numbers of patrons from the surrounding areas. Le Club d'Esclavage was a scrupulously monitored establishment catering to adults interested in the BDSM scene. Whether you were a novice interested in participating in a little 'slap and tickle,' or a 'whip me, beat me, call me trash' hardcore enthusiast, Le Club d'Esclavage offered something to whet any appetite.

The owner of the club remained a mystery. His or her identity had never been revealed, and all media correspondence regarding the popular establishment was conducted through its manager, Troy Simon. Troy, a vigilant observer, demanded all guests and employees follow strict guidelines while patronizing the club. First and foremost all arrangements of play were to be consensual, no bestiality, no pain infliction for the sake of inflicting pain, no blood play, all engaging partners must practice safe play at all times. And above all else, have a great fucking time! It's just sex, after all.

During the grand opening, Troy was quoted as saying, "The owner would like to make one thing very clear. When you cross the threshold into Le Club d'Esclavage, it is your desire to participate completely in our manner of play, and such will be expected of you."

Within the glossy pages of the magazine Dani found herself more than curious about what went on inside the walls of the club. Each time she read the article, she couldn't control her body's response to the words and pictures on the pages. Never before had her body reacted with such fierce sexual need. To say she was intrigued would be an understatement.

Scooping up the magazine, she flipped to the article once again and smiled. She'd read it so many times the corners of the pages were dog-eared.

"You know what, Lady Godiva," she said to the fat calico cat, lazily sauntering through the open sliding door. "I think I want a piece of that lifestyle."

CHAPTER 1

Sweat poured off Mike Ranger's body as he finished the last set of presses. After placing the barbell in the holder, he sat up and reached for the water bottle at his foot. Each morning his day began by spending two hours in the employees' exercise room. What he would have preferred was to start the days by getting sweaty beneath his bed sheets with a vivacious brunette with big, brown eyes.

A curvy brunette was Mike's biggest weakness.

It had been some time since he'd had the privilege of sharing the warmth of a woman's body. Three long years. Regardless of the fact he worked in the hottest BDSM club within a hundred mile radius, every night Mike crawled into his king-size bed alone.

The door to the gym opened and Max Renfrew, the club's owner, entered. Mike glanced over, then rose to his feet.

"Hey," Max said in greeting. "How are you?"

"Great," Mike replied. "You ready to run?"

Max nodded on his way across the room toward the state of the art sound system. "You bet." He slipped AC/DC's Black Ice CD into the carousel, and cranked up the volume. "Five miles work for you today?"

"Let's make it ten." Mike walked toward one of the four

treadmills set up along one wall. "I've got some tension to work off."

Max stepped onto the machine beside Mike and grinned. "Running isn't going to burn off that kind of tension, my friend."

"Yeah, well, it's all I got right now."

Max chuckled and keyed in his settings. "Don't sweat it, big man. I may have something in the works that just might help you out."

Mike grimaced while he programmed the computer of the machine he was using. "No, no, no. Don't bother setting me up with somebody's sister, or a friend of a friend. I've got a hard-on, yes, but I'm not hard up."

Max reached over and punched the 'start' signal on Mike's treadmill, catching him off guard. With a curse, he stumbled half a dozen steps before regaining his balance.

"Asshole," Mike bit out before settling into a stride.

In silence the two men ran their ten miles before parting ways. After a hot shower in his apartment on the premises, Mike strolled into the main room of the club. Being mid-afternoon the club was empty. Bright fluorescent lights overhead illuminated the vast open space.

Deirdre, the head of the bartending staff, was taking stock before opening for the night. The woman was most men's wet dream come to life. Long blond curls, luscious curves, infectious laugh and personality, blessed with the body of a swimsuit model. The bombshell exuded sexual appeal at its premium. And there wasn't a man on the planet who stood a snowball's chance in hell of getting into her pants. In her opinion the only thing men were good for was to deposit a load of sperm into a Dixie cup for women to use to artificially inseminate themselves. That and to annihilate "icky, creepy, crawly bugs with lots of legs."

"Hey there, Dee," Mike said as he slid onto a stool in front of the marble topped bar. "You're in early."

"Hiya, Mikey."

Deirdre was one of the few people permitted to call him 'Mikey.' Actually, Mike never had the nerve to correct her. Despite her five-feet-nothing frame Deirdre wasn't someone to be messed with. One time in particular he recalled the petite fireball throwing some brute out on his ear after she caught him slipping ruffies into a woman's drink while she boogied with friends on the dance floor. Mike was appreciative that when others were around Deirdre used plain old 'Mike' to address him

"My new guy closed last night, and I'm checking to make sure he did everything I'd asked," she said.

At the end of the hall leading to the employee suites the deadbolt lock tripped and the heavy steel door swung open. Two men approached the bar, Troy Simon, the club manager, along with his lover, Ransom Seager.

"Afternoon, Deirdre. Mike," Troy said.

"Hi guys," Ransom greeted as well.

Small talk was exchanged among the quartet as a half hour passed. The front door swung open, and the sounds of cars whizzing up and down the street out front filled the emptiness of the club. The casual conversation the co-workers shared stopped as a voluptuous brunette sashayed through the door. The seductive sway of her hips produced a groan from deep within Mike's chest.

"Mmm, I'd like a piece of that," Deirdre uttered just loud enough for the three men to hear. "By the way, sorry boss. I didn't the lock the door after I came in."

"It's all right, Deirdre," Troy assured her.

Inch by delectable inch Mike's eyes scaled the woman's lush frame. The monster between his legs raged, demanding he toss her over his shoulder and cart her up to his suite. He wanted to tie her spread eagle atop his bed and with his tongue worship every molecule that made up her body.

"Hands off," Mike growled. The possession he heard in his tone made him straighten on the stool.

Deirdre snickered and went back to counting the bottles of booze lining the counter.

Troy stood and, with a confident stride, approached the gorgeous woman who'd entered. "I'm sorry, miss, but we're not open to the public for another couple of hours."

"Actually, Mr. Simon, I was hoping for a moment of your time," she said. Although she spoke to Troy, her big brown eyes focused on Mike. "May we speak in private?"

With a nod Troy led the woman toward the back of the club. Mike clenched his fists on his thighs, watching the two disappear down the hall to the office.

* * * *

Dani was escorted down a long hallway. Step by step her mind raced with naughty thoughts of the man seated at the bar. Though there were two men sitting side by side, her focus had been on the largest.

[181]

The man was huge while seated, and she wondered how intimidating he would be when standing. His broad shoulders had to span four feet across at least, and the black t-shirt he wore served only to enhance the bulge of muscle beneath. Dark, untamed waves had her fingertips itching to run through them. To fist her fingers in his hair while she held him to her breast, or better yet, lower. His brown eyes had roamed up and down her small body. Well, she wasn't particularly "small." Standing around five-one, her breasts were a little too big for her frame, her hips were on the wide side, as was her butt, but she did have a tiny waist. The man's expression had been one of hunger as he appeared to undress her with his eyes.

Perhaps she should have been appalled at the way he'd blatantly ogled her, but Dani was anything but. Hell, she'd been ogling right back. Visions of straddling his powerful thighs played in her mind's eye. Due to his incredible size she wondered what sort of monster he was packing in those blue jeans. What kind of lover would he be? Would the touch of his large hands be rough and demanding, or gentle and persuasive?

As she imagined the stroke of his fingers, a shiver raced through her body from the tips of her toes to the top of her head. What would his full lips feel like pressed against her flesh? Suckling her breasts? Sampling her pussy? The sudden tightening of her nipples stole her breath. She envisioned the wet slide of his tongue in all the right places. How would he feel about experimenting, trying different positions, using implements? Would he allow her to tie him up and make him submit to her newfound cravings?

The bundle of nerves between her legs swelled, creating a delightfully agonizing friction with every step she took. Would he tie her up, and make her submit to him? The response of her body to the thoughts alone was almost enough to make her stop walking, lean against the wall for support, and come right there.

"Here we are." The man behind her interrupted her x-rated thoughts as they arrived at a closed door at the end of the corridor. He reached for the knob and opened the door.

Dani stepped through the doorway into a room larger than her entire apartment. The simple furnishings depicted a lounge area as opposed to an office. The atmosphere inside was one hundred percent alpha male.

To her immediate right were three black, leather sofas. Two facing each other, the third facing a large gas fireplace built into the wall. The centerpiece of the square setup was an octagon-shaped glass coffee table.

In the middle of the room a pool table displayed the remains of a game left abandoned. A dozen or so balls, an equal number of solids and stripes, littered the felt surface, and a cue leaned against one of the polished wooden sides.

A small wet bar, similar to the one in the main area of the club, sat in one corner, and in the opposite corner stood a tiny, beat-up, old desk cluttered with paper. Behind the tattered piece of furniture were several black filing cabinets. Not a single picture hung on any of the four windowless walls.

"Please, have a seat," Troy said, motioning to one of the sofas.

[183]

"May I offer you something to drink?"

"Uh, no, thank you," she replied. "I'm fine."

Taking a seat in the middle of the closest couch, Dani sat with her legs closed tight, hands folded on her lap. For the first time since deciding to pay Mr. Simon a visit, she found herself nervous.

Across from her Troy sat down in one corner, crossed his left ankle over his right knee, and rested his arms along the back and side of the big, comfy couch. Dark gray eyes studied her, his expression controlled and unreadable. Troy Simon was handsome. There was no question about that. He exuded dominance, and power, and Dani had little doubt women would submit to him with nothing more than a look.

"What can I do for you, Miss..."

Dani cleared her throat before answering. She wondered if she still had a voice as his gaze appeared to be seeking out her deepest, darkest secrets.

"Danielle Miller," she replied. "My friends call me Dani. I'm sorry, up until a minute ago I was feeling pretty confident about meeting with you. Now I'm embarrassed to admit I'm nervous."

"There's no reason to be nervous, Dani," Troy said smoothly. A slight grin curled his lips on one side. "I don't bite."

She wasn't so sure about that.

"Now tell me, to what do I owe the pleasure of your visit?"

"Well, I read the article published in the magazine, *In the Know*," she began. "And I'm intrigued."

Troy nodded, his eyes remained focused.

Again, she cleared her throat, and then continued. "It's more than a curiosity, Mr. Simon—"

"Call me Troy."

Butterflies filled her belly, and she felt her cheeks heat. "Thank you. Troy," she repeated. "When I read the article, or when I'm doing a little research on the BDSM scene my body reacts in ways I've never felt before, and—"

"How do you react?" Uncrossing his legs, Troy leaned forward, resting his forearms on his knees. He still looked comfortable, now a little intimidating, but not in a threatening manner.

"P-pardon?"

"Tell me how your body reacts to the words you read, the pictures you see when you conduct your research."

The tone in his voice sent a shiver coursing through her body. Though not as keenly stimulated as she became thinking about the man at the bar, she realized she was turned on.

"Well, I become aroused, and feel things in parts of my body I never knew existed."

"Do your nipples get hard?" he asked.

Dani inhaled sharply. "Y-yes," she replied after a handful of seconds.

"Do the muscles of your pussy begin to throb and ache?"

Dani nodded, but couldn't bring herself to speak.

"Tell me," he commanded in a soft voice.

Immediately she imagined the big man seated in the bar, and envisioned doing the things she'd read about with him. Her body ignited.

"My nipples are hard, my breasts swollen and they ache. My skin is tingling like thousands of needles are piercing my flesh. I'm beginning to perspire," she said, studying his expression. Was the description of her arousal turning him on? She learned nothing as she watched him listening to her.

As she continued Dani's breath grew harsh, raspy, and her body was on fire. She was close to the edge of losing control, seated across from a total stranger, telling him how hot she got thinking about the BDSM scene and more specifically the man seated in the bar. "My p-pussy is pulsing, and I-I'm wet. The need for release is so bad I want to touch myself. It doesn't matter where I am. I need."

"Your eyes are flickering with a lick of desire as you speak. Your description carries too much emotion to have been brought on by the article itself. Only an attraction to another would bring on a confession such as that," he said.

Taken aback by his statement Dani replayed what she'd said, and gasped. She'd spoken her feelings of arousal in present tense. She had just sat before a total stranger and told him how hot she was. How she was on the verge of coming right there on his leather sofa.

"Tell me who you are thinking of. Who has made you so wet?" The smooth tone of his voice brought the answer from her lips. She couldn't have stopped it if she'd tried.

"The man at the bar," she whispered without hesitation.

"Which man?" he asked, his lips lifting in a grin again.

"The b-big man. With dark hair."

In a soft, confident voice Troy asked, "What position do you see yourself in, Dani?"

"All of them," she replied in a breathless rush.

A low chuckle brought her back to reality. "What I mean is do you see yourself in a position of dominance, or submission?"

After bringing her libido under control, well somewhat, Dani replied, "Dominatrix."

He chuckled, and Dani fought the urge to bark out asking him what he found so funny. As she replayed the last few minutes in her mind, she realized she'd completely given in to the submissive role.

Damn it! In silence she fumed. She'd just blown her chance to be trained in domination by the Master by being so damned submissive. Dani believed she had what it took to be a Domme. She knew she needed guidance and direction, and who better to teach her than Troy Simon, a well respected and experienced Dom in the community.

As the silence deepened between them his gaze held hers. Beneath her the leather creaked as she squirmed under the weight of his scrutiny. Several moments passed before Troy again spoke.

"I will teach you," he finally said.

Dani blew out a breath she'd been holding, anxiously awaiting his answer. "Really?"

Troy stood and held his hand out to her. Placing her hand in his, she felt her confidence strengthen. "Our exercise a moment ago tells me unequivocally you have submissive tendencies, Dani. Are you certain you have what it takes to switch?"

"Yes," she replied without hesitation. In that moment, the big burly hunk seated at the bar when she entered flashed in her mind.

[187]

When her eyes met his a short time earlier her body felt as if it'd been lit on fire. Low in her belly a spasm shot even lower to the sudden pulsing between her thighs. Not wanting to be outdone by the other over-stimulated erogenous zones, her nipples began to throb in time with the muscles in her pussy.

Thatta' girl, her aroused subconscious cheered. *Go for the biggest guy in the place!*

She wanted to tame the man in the bar.

"We will start tomorrow," Troy said, and led her toward the door.

As they walked back through the corridor Dani's mind raced in a thousand different directions. The meeting left her with many questions, but she didn't know where to begin.

"I don't have any stuff," she said. "You know equipment, or toys.

"I have everything you could possibly need," Troy replied as they stepped back into the bar area.

Dani's breath caught as the dark-haired man at the bar spun around, his eyes settling on her. Hunger. There was no mistaking the glint of animal lust in his gaze. A chill raced the length of Dani's spine, and her skin prickled. Fighting off the urge to dash to the man and lick every inch of his hulking body, Dani drew several deep breaths as she and Troy approached the trio at bar.

"Gang, this is Dani," Troy began. "She'll be spending some time around here. Dani, this is Ransom," Troy said, and the blond seated beside the dark-haired god nodded.

"Nice to meet you, Dani," he said.

"That's Deirdre behind the bar. She manages our wait staff."

"Pleasure." The blond woman purred.

Finally Troy came to the man who rendered her speechless with that look in his eyes.

"This is Mike, our head of security."

"Hi," Dani squeaked out softly.

"Dani," Mike said. The deep timbre of his voice wrapped around her in a seductive embrace full of promise.

Troy cleared his throat as the silence became deafening. "Until tomorrow, Dani," he said and placed his hand against her back, escorting her toward the door.

A low growl came from the bar, and her body shuddered at the savage sound. Dani refused to turn around. Afraid if she did she'd hurl herself into Mike's arms and beg him to ravage her right there on the marble topped surface.

A throaty chuckle carried to her ears as the distance grew between her and the others. "Easy does it, big man," she heard Ransom say.

"Tomorrow, Dani, all you need to bring is your enthusiasm, and willingness to submit," Troy said as he followed her outside.

"But I want to be the one in control," she began to argue.

The look Troy gave her made Dani drop her gaze to the center of his chest. With the tip of his index finger Troy lifted Dani's chin until her eyes met his.

"I will teach you everything you want to learn, but *I* am always the Master. Do you understand?"

Dani nodded, but remained silent.

"I must hear the words, Dani."

"Yes, Troy, I understand."

"Good. I'll see you tomorrow."

* * * *

Mike was off his barstool like a shot and storming toward Troy when he walked back into the club.

"What the fuck was that all about?" he barked out. "I'm pretty sure I said hands off."

The raised brow and smirk Troy gave stopped Mike in his tracks. "That certainly didn't apply to me, my friend."

"It meant everybody," Mike snarled.

"Ease up, big man," Troy said, slinging his arm around Mike's shoulders. "The little lady is looking to be trained. I agreed to tutor her."

The blood drained from Mike's body, rushing to his feet. He felt his massive frame waver. There was no way in hell *anyone* but he would put their hands on his woman. *My woman?* Mike drew to a halt, and tipped his head to the side in consideration. Never before in his life had he been prepared to stake his claim on a woman. Yet that curvy, little brunette triggered something in him he'd never experienced before.

"You all right, Mike?" Deirdre asked, her well-groomed brow furrowing in concerned. "You're white as a sheet."

Yes, my woman.

"Mike?" Troy's voice sounded beside him.

My woman.

[190]

"If she wants to be trained, I'll do it," Mike growled.

Amusement flickered in Troy's eyes, and Mike grimaced. Knowing Troy as long as he had, Mike knew damn well his friend was up to something, and it wasn't going to go in Mike's favor until Troy was good and ready.

"Don't sweat it, big guy," Troy said, patting him heartily on his back. "I'll handle this trainee, and you can have the next one."

A primal sound erupted from deep within him, and Mike fought the urge to take a swing at Troy.

"Okay." Troy slapped his hands together. With a grin first to Mike, he then turned his attention to Deirdre, then Ransom and said, "I'm going to need an assistant to help me with my new sub. Anyone interested?"

Deirdre and Ransom both raised their hands eagerly chanting, "Pick me, pick me." Mike grew livid, certain steam was about to shoot from his ears.

"Ransom," Troy announced.

"Ahh, shucks." Deirdre pouted from behind the bar. "You always choose him. It's just not fair."

"We begin tomorrow," Troy said.

In an instant Mike saw red.

"You better run, lover boy," Ransom's voice chided as Mike took a step forward. "The big man looks pissed."

Troy turned to see Mike take another step toward him. "Come on, Mike," Troy said in a playful tone. "I'm not into women. She'll be safe."

At the moment, Mike didn't give a shit. "Run, little man," was all he said.

Troy blew out a hearty belly laugh and took off down the hall toward his office.

"I'm going to kill him," Mike said evenly, his fists clenched tight at his sides. "Very, very slowly. And with a great deal of pain."

Ransom rose from his barstool and crossed the room. Resting his hand on Mike's shoulder, he chuckled. "She lit the fuse, huh?"

Mike nodded.

"She'll be in good hands."

"She should be in *my* hands."

CHAPTER 2

Standing under the hot spray of the shower, Dani anxiously wondered what Troy had in store for her first day of training. She hadn't slept a single wink the night before. Her anticipation level skyrocketed through the roof.

First off, thoughts of Mike triggered her arousal the moment her naked form slid beneath her cool cotton sheets, and there'd been no stopping it. With the help of her trusty vibrator she'd reached orgasm twice, yet only achieved mild satisfaction. She wondered what his big, strong hands would feel like caressing over her heated flesh. Would his full lips be soft and teasing as they sought out her secrets? Or would they be confident and firm, demanding her complete submission?

The last thought had her replaying Troy's appraisal of her having submissive tendencies. She refused to accept his deduction. She intended to be in complete and utter control. Under Troy's tutelage she would learn how to make Mike submit to her.

But what if he wasn't the submissive sort? Dani hadn't thought of that when she first laid eyes on him. She'd seen the heat of desire in his expression when he looked at her. There was no denying his interest. Maybe he was a Dom, and presented with the opportunity perhaps it would be his intention to make her submit.

Reaching down, she shut the water off and pushed the vinyl curtain to one side. Stepping over the side of the tub, she grabbed a fluffy bath towel and wrapped up her wet hair. She pulled a second around her body.

Dani crossed her bedroom, stopping at the foot of her bed to take stock of the lingerie littering the surface. Troy hadn't mentioned that she should wear anything specific, but if she wanted to be taken seriously as a Domme, she needed to look the part.

Loosening the plush fabric on her head, she towel dried her hair. A moment later, she decided on a red leather bustier she'd bought the day before, after Troy agreed to tutor her. Dropping both towels to the floor, she reached for the sexy garment and wrapped it around her torso. After lacing the front closed, leaving a teasing amount of breast showing, she stepped into a matching thong.

To complete the ensemble, sheer stockings were pulled up her legs and the lacy band at the top fastened to a garter belt. The final accessory was thigh-high, black vinyl boots with a five-inch heel.

A smile curled her lips as she studied her reflection in the mirror. "Not bad," she mused aloud as she turned this way and that, taking in every angle. She wondered what Mike would think.

* * * *

As Troy had instructed the day before Dani pressed the buzzer on the left side of the door marked *STAFF*. With nervous anticipation she waited, willing her anxieties to take a hike. This was what she wanted, she reminded herself. Dani jumped when the deadbolt clicked. The door swung open, and she was greeted by Troy.

"An early bird," he said. "I like that. Come in."

"Thank you," Dani replied as he stepped back and she entered.

"We'll be going upstairs to my personal suite." He motioned toward a staircase off to one side. "Right this way."

As she climbed the stairs, Dani realized she was disappointed. She'd been hoping Mike would answer the door. It also added to her disappointment that she'd come in the back way rather than through the front where she stood a chance of seeing him.

Since the club wasn't open to the public this early in the afternoon Dani wondered where he was, and what he was doing. Despite the heated visual caress he gave her the day before, it was conceivable he had a significant other. The thought made Dani's heart plummet.

"Here we are." Troy's voice broke into her daydream, reminding her the training she wanted to experience was about to commence. He pushed the heavy steel door open and ushered her inside.

"Let me take your coat," Troy said, holding his hand out. "You won't need it for a while."

Remembering all she wore underneath was a red leather bustier, she hesitated, but only for a moment. Pulling the belt from around her waist, she unbuttoned the front of the light-weight, tan trench coat and slid the material over her shoulders. Standing nearly naked in front of Troy, a sudden surge of self-consciousness assailed her. Dani dropped her gaze to the floor.

"Sexy," he said, taking a moment to look her over. A smile curled his lips. "Excellent choice of attire."

"Thank you."

"Come." He held his hand out to her. "Our sessions will take place in the playroom." Troy led Dani through the living room area and down a short hall to a closed door.

"Are you ready?" he asked, reaching for the knob.

Dani nodded.

"You must use words now," he said. "In order for you to be a confident Mistress for your slave, you must use words. More importantly, you must insist your slave uses words as well. Between a Mistress, or Master, and their submissive, verbal communication is key."

"I understand."

"It is of utmost importance that your submissive's safety always remains your first priority. Yes, though it is true that pleasure can be found in pain, your slave must feel safe in your hands. He or she must never question that you will keep them safe no matter what manner of play you engage in. Do you understand?"

"Yes," Dani replied.

"Very well. Let's begin."

Troy pushed the door open and, with his hand against her back, encouraged Dani to step inside. Once she did, and her eyes scanned the large room, a soft gasp escaped her. On her drive to the club she hadn't been sure what to expect, but this wasn't it.

Equipment of various sizes and shapes were set up throughout the room. There were items resembling a cross, a bench, and stands. Dani could imagine them in use. Then there were other structures and devices that looked right out of medieval times, which she wasn't certain she wanted to see in use.

Shelves lined the mirrored walls, and upon them were a variety of sex toys and bottles of lotions, potions and lubes. From her research of adult novelties, and her own personal experience visiting sex stores, she recognized most of the toys on display. There were an array of butt plugs in various sizes, dildos, and vibrators similar to one she had at home. As well as an assortment of restraints made of metals, fabrics, some with buckles or Velcro. Hanging along the far wall she spotted an impressive collection of paddles and floggers of different styles and textures.

In the center of the room knelt the blond man from the day before. Though he was handsome and possessed a physique most men might kill for, he didn't really turn her on. She was curious as to why that was. She'd read about the submissive pose he was in—kneeling on the floor, hands resting on his thighs palms up, eyes downcast—but what caught her off guard was...

"He's naked," Dani blurted.

"Of course," Troy replied. "He's supposed to be."

"But...but..." She couldn't think of how to finish.

Sure, she'd seen naked men before, but for the first time since she decided to embark on this adventure she wasn't so sure she could follow through. Yes, she wanted to be trained by Troy Simon to be a Domme, but the man she wanted as her submissive was Mike. Dani didn't know if she could be trained using a man she felt little attraction toward. Ransom was attractive, but Dani's mind and body were affected in all the right places by another man. And wasn't that supposed to be part of the appeal of the lifestyle?

"Surely you aren't offended by his nakedness?"

"Good Lord, no," Dani admitted. "Don't get me wrong, he's hot. I just thought..."

"You are his Mistress. It is a sign of respect to you that your slave acknowledges his submission by displaying himself to you without barriers. His body belongs to you. He is yours."

"O-okay," Dani replied. Mike came to mind again, and she voiced the reservations she felt. "But shouldn't I be working with someone I feel, you know, something for? Isn't that part of it?"

"Yes. In time, when you are ready, we will bring in another. For now, and the purposes of our sessions, Ransom will be your slave, and in that role, he will follow your instruction without question. Together we will aid in your training, but it will be your willingness to learn that will heighten your experience."

"I understand," she said.

"Excellent. Now, do you recall our discussion in the other room regarding your submissive's safety?"

"It is to be my number one priority. My slave must feel safe in my hands."

"Good. I know you've been researching the lifestyle. What do you do now?"

"My slave needs to choose a safe word. Something he will say if he doesn't feel safe, or is experiencing pain which is not enjoyable. Speaking his safe word will stop our play immediately."

"Very good," Troy praised. "Let's begin."

* * * *

When the session ended Troy helped Dani release the restraints around Ransom's wrists. "Nice job," Troy said, and pressed a kiss to Ransom's lips. "Both of you."

The kiss between the two men took her by surprise. "You're lovers?"

Ransom crossed the playroom and snatched a towel and a robe hanging from a hook on the wall. "Yup," he replied, wrapping the towel around his waist.

"Does that bother you?" Troy asked, taking the robe from Ransom and helping Dani to slip it on.

She shook her head at his question, and synched the belt. "Not at all. It's just that you two give off serious alpha vibes. I didn't consider you might be lovers."

"Well, you shouldn't buy into the stereotype, sweetie," Ransom said, winking in her direction.

"Yeah, you're right," Dani said. "Sorry. I hope I didn't offend you."

"Not in the least," Troy replied. "Now come, let's relax in the living room and discuss our session over a glass of wine."

Once seated on an overstuffed suede sofa in the living room, Troy began. "You did very well today, Dani. You will make a worthy Mistress for the right man. I imagine very soon."

"Really? You think so?" she asked, sounding a little too eager.

"I'd say." Ransom chuckled. "Today was only day one, but you're a natural with a paddle. Tanned my cheeks nicely."

She laughed. "I'm sorry."

"Don't be sorry. I loved it. You paddle like a pro. You need to work on your technique with the flogger, but given some practice, you'll ace that too."

"Ransom's right, you're a natural, and your willingness to learn is exceptional. Your confidence will strengthen with each session, and before you know it, you Miss Miller will be Mistress of your own domain."

"Thanks, guys." Dani felt herself beaming. "I really had fun. When I wasn't concentrating so hard."

"We covered a lot of ground today. Gave you a lot to absorb," Troy said. "You did well."

Dani finished her wine and set the empty glass on the coffee table. "I should probably get going. I'm expected at the diner for the dinner rush."

Ransom glanced at the clock on the wall. "Shame to cut this short, but the club will be opening in a couple of hours, so we should get downstairs ourselves."

"Let's get your coat, and I'll walk you out," Troy said, and offered her his hand.

As they reached the bottom of the stairs, Dani stopped short when she spotted Mike leaning against the wall near the door.

"Oh my," she gasped.

Dark brown eyes focused on her as he pulled himself from the wall. Standing full height he towered over her. He was huge. Dani guessed he had to be six-five, six-six easily, and probably tipped the scales at close to three hundred pounds. The man was muscle on top of muscle, but not in a 'body builder on steroids' sort of way.

A lucky white t-shirt molded to his chest like a second skin, emphasizing the ripples of an eight-pack set of abs. Pectoral muscles tensed, drawing her eyes to the dark shading of his areolas and the tip of erect nipples straining against the fabric.

Suddenly, she became uncomfortably wet between her legs.

"Hello, Dani," he said in a deep voice. The husky tone ignited sparks low in her belly.

"Mike," she said in raspy whisper.

"Good first day?"

Dani swallowed the lump lodged in her throat and felt her knees weaken. She nodded, and then replied, "Only one thing would have made it more fulfilling."

Good God! Where did that come from?

A feral grin curled his full lips, and the heat of lust in his eyes deepened. "Oh, yeah? What's that?"

The lilt in his voice made Dani wonder if Mike was reading her thoughts. You! She wanted to scream out.

Sliding his hands into his front pockets brought her gaze straight to the straining bulge at the top of his powerful thighs.

"Oh God, I-I—"

"I, for one, need to get to work," Troy said, pulling her thoughts back before she threw herself in Mike's arms. The hand at the small of her back encouraged her to move forward. "We'll see you tomorrow," he said.

"Um, right. W-What's on tap then?"

"A review of today's lessons. Then we'll see."

"Okay. Well, goodbye then," she said, stealing a glance at Mike over Troy's shoulder.

"Sweet dreams," Mike called out.

* * * *

Mike watched as Troy made sure Dani got into her car safely and drove away. When he locked the door and turned around, Mike blocked his path to the bar area. Troy smiled a knowing grin.

"What was she wearing under the coat?" Mike asked in a strained voice.

"Red leather bustier with matching thong panties. Garter and hose. The boots were a nice touch."

Mike's body trembled as he envisioned Dani standing before him dressed as Troy described. His balls were on the verge of rupturing from the pressure building in them. "Jesus."

"Ransom says she's a natural with a paddle."

Taking several deep breaths to calm his raging libido, Mike sighed and rolled his head from side to side. "As a matter of record, you do know I am going to kill you, right?"

"Yup, slowly and painfully," Troy replied. Slipping past him, he grinned. "I heard. It'll have to wait until another time. Tonight we've got a club to run."

* * * *

After their session Dani sat with Ransom and Troy, as they had done following each training, and discussed the day's experience. Something had been niggling at her since the first day, but she wasn't sure how to bring it up. Ransom was a great sub to work with, and she was thankful for his support and encouragement. Troy was an exceptional teacher. He rewarded and corrected in the same tone of voice, yet Dani always knew where she stood with him. His direction always began as instructional before they moved on.

Anatomy was the topic of discussion during one day's training. Dani found this quite interesting. Troy and Ransom gave her a lesson on muscles groups, and how the different pieces of equipment in the playroom affected those muscles. She allowed them to strap her to the various apparatuses, putting her in positions where she could experience the encounter to its fullest extent.

Not once during her training did Dani have sex with Ransom. In fact, there had been no sexual contact between them at all. Though he performed his role as her submissive naked, and her scarcely dressed, there had been nothing sexual between them. Ransom never even achieved an erection when they played. Even when she tried that new thing earlier. She knew he enjoyed it, she could see it in his eyes.

"What are you thinking, Dani?" Troy asked. "You're concentrating so hard steam is rising off the top of your head."

"Really?"

Both men laughed.

"No, not literally. What's on your mind?"

"Why don't you get hard?" she asked Ransom.

An instant grin curled his lips. "Don't take this the wrong way, doll, but you aren't my type."

"Hmm."

"What's with the 'hmm'? Listen you're cute as hell, but beyond that, I'm not attracted to you sexually," he replied.

"Okay."

"Do you get turned on while we're practicing?" he asked.

Shaking her head, she gave a single shoulder shrug. "No, I don't. Not even a little bit."

Except when I'm picturing Mike in your place.

"Your brows are still furrowed," Troy said.

"Well, isn't that what I mentioned the first day? In order for this to be all that it can be, shouldn't I be working with someone I'm attracted to? Someone who is attracted to me? Isn't that what it's all about?"

Like maybe me and Mike.

"Yes on all accounts," Troy replied.

"Don't get me wrong, I like working with Ransom, he makes me comfortable so I can put into practice what I've learned."

"I feel the same way, Dani. You've come a long way in the short time we've spent together," Ransom said. "You're very good at what you do."

"Think I'm ready to be with someone else?" she asked

"You're dumping me?" Ransom gasped in feigned shock, and then chuckled.

Dani laughed. "You'll always be my first."

"If you are confident, then yes, I think you're ready," Troy said.

"Cool! Do I choose someone? Or will you decide?" she asked, directing her question to Troy.

"I have someone in mind," he answered. "A Master, or Mistress, doesn't choose their submissive, it's the other way around."

"You're right. I was so caught up in the fun of it, I kinda' forgot that. Some Mistress, huh? That's an important aspect to overlook."

"You've only been at it a few weeks," Ransom reminded her. "Don't be too hard on yourself."

Dani was disappointed. She'd hope the choice would be hers to make, because she had the perfect person in mind. Despite getting tongue-tied when around Mike, Dani knew once she had him where she wanted him, the sparks would fly. She wasn't being egotistical, just confident with what she'd learned.

Nearly every day she came to the club, she crossed paths with Mike, though they were never alone. Troy was always with her, whether it was when she arrived or when she left.

The hunger in Mike's eyes when he looked at her sent her body into orbit. With just a simple glance the man made her panties wet. She'd never felt so tortured in all her life as she felt day in and day out seeing Mike and not being able to touch him.

On her first day of training Troy said she was not permitted to come to the club unless it was for a session. Several times over the month she had been tempted to defy his direction, and head to the club just to see Mike.

"You're really into deep contemplation today, Dani. What's on your mind now?" Ransom asked.

"I was thinking about what you said about me not being your type."

"Hold on, I said you were cute—"

"Save it, blondie. You said it and you can't take it back," she teased. "I know the two of you are lovers, but have you ever been with women?"

"Yes, we've both been with women in the past. We choose to be in a committed gay relationship now."

"Stop pissing around, Dani-girl," Troy said. "What is it you're trying to say?"

"I have a friend, and I was thinking about what you said about me having submissive tendencies."

"Yeah?" Troy shifted on the chair across from her.

"Well, Meg's like that. Submissive, I mean. I can see it in her face. Anyhow, I was wondering since you guys are teaching me to explore both my dominant and submissive sides, maybe you can show her how to embrace hers."

When neither man spoke for several moments Dani regretted bringing Megan's name up. But after her first meeting with Troy she immediately recognized her friend's submissive nature, and wanted nothing more than for her to explore it.

"It's not a set up, guys, honest. I know you two are in love, and I'm not suggesting... Wait... Oh, I don't know what I'm suggesting. Sorry. It's pretty bold of me to ask you to help my friend tap into her submissive side, when you've already done so much for me."

"It's just that it's not an undertaking to be looked upon lightly,

Dani," Troy said. "As I've told you before a sub chooses their Master, not the other way around. A submissive must want to explore that part of themselves. Does your friend want to?"

"I don't know. I don't think she realizes she is one."

"That's the first thing you should find out," Troy said. "You know we're always here to answer any questions you have."

"Yeah, I know." She glanced down at her watch. "Damn, I've got to go. It's my mom and dad's date night, so I've got to head into work for closing time."

* * * *

Mike was sitting on the same barstool he'd been on when Dani had arrived for her session. Four hours had passed, and there he still sat, his eyes glued to the door leading to the staff apartments.

Since the first day Dani Miller graced the club with her stunning presence, Mike had been forbidden to escort her to her car, or to go to her place of employment, or to her apartment while she was training.

Troy's *orders* had made him furious. After some consideration however, Mike relented. Hell, her training wouldn't go on forever, and when it was over maybe she'd be interested in taming his beast. He could only hope.

"Aww, Mikey, I hate seeing you so down." Deirdre interrupted his pity party. "But think how much fun Dani will be when Troy finishes with her."

Mike growled in response.

"Come on, you're not still sore about that, are you?"

He scowled at her.

"You big baby," she teased.

The door to the private suites opened, and Dani and Troy emerged. Immediately, her eyes searched the bar to settle on him. His cock hardened in an instant, and he felt lightheaded. A flirtatious grin curled her full, kissable lips, and her brown eyes sparkled. If Mike wasn't mistaken, they flickered with desire, and need.

A sideways glance from Troy stopped him from jumping off his stool, racing to her, tossing her up over his shoulder, and stealing away to his lair.

"Come on, Mikey, you aren't going to let the boss man push your buttons, are you?" Deirdre taunted near his ear. "You can take him, you're bigger than he is. Go and claim your woman."

"Can I get an orange juice, please?" Mike grumbled.

"Kinda' early for the hard stuff, isn't it?" She laughed.

Just like every day, Troy escorted Dani out of the club and to her car. Once she walked out the door, leaving him with his x-rated thoughts, Mike turned on his stool and watched Deirdre preparing for the busy night ahead. A few minutes later, Troy returned and sat on the stool beside Mike.

"May I have a soda, Deirdre, please," Troy said, and offered a wink to the scantily clad blonde behind the bar.

"Sure thing, boss," she replied with a sexy grin.

Mike felt Troy's eyes on him, could even feel the smugness in his grin.

"I'm. Going. To. Kill. You."

"Yeah, yeah. Slowly and painfully, I've heard," Troy said.

"Listen, hold that thought, because this is your lucky day, my friend."

"Don't toy with me, Simon. I'm not in the mood."

"Thanks, doll," Troy said as Deirdre set a glass in front of him. "I'm serious, Mike."

"My lucky day, huh? Why's that?"

"Well, as much fun as my Mistress in training is having with Ransom, she would like to try her hand with another."

The beast between his legs took over the final thread of Mike's control on his libido. Four weeks and three days he'd watched the woman who haunted his dreams disappear with Troy for training. It didn't matter that Mike knew sex wasn't part of the sessions. It still ate at him that Ransom was the one assisting Troy, when it should be him.

"There's no question she likes to take the lead, but she's got sub flowing through her veins," Troy said.

"Is that so," Mike replied, and whimpered inwardly at the strain he heard in his voice.

Troy's knowing, deep chuckle only added to Mike's discomfort. He knew damn well Troy knew he was more than willing to offer himself up as Dani's new play toy.

"I take it the 'big bad Dom' in you isn't opposed to playing sub for the right Mistress?"

"I'd give my left nut for the opportunity."

Troy laughed. "Since day one you've made your interest abundantly clear, Mike. I've seen the way you look at her, and I knew you'd be agreeable. I promise it won't cost you a nut, but consider yourself forewarned—she does have a fascination with the 'boys.'"

It sounded too damned good to be true. Mike loved his balls toyed with. "How so?" he asked, attempting to control the strain in his voice.

"Today she asked to try something she'd read about. So she tied an intricate knot around Ransom's sac and hung a hefty weight from the end."

This time Mike didn't even bother to stifle his groan of his arousal. Dani could tie him up and bull whip him senseless if she so desired. Mike never considered himself a true Dom in the BDSM world. The practice of dominance in his past sexual experiences seemed to be based on his physical size. He was a large man, standing six-five and tipping the scales around two-hundred-seventy-five pounds. During his junior year of high school he'd joined the wrestling team and won numerous championships throughout high school and college.

It seemed as if the women he'd been with expected him to take the lead in the bedroom. Mike's deepest desire was for the woman to take control. To turn 'big Mike' into her sex slave. The thought of Dani Miller being that woman kept him up at night. Literally.

"Christ, his nuggets turned deep purple in an instant," Troy said, interrupting Mike's thoughts. "If it hadn't been for the sexy sparkle in Ransom's eyes, I would have made her untie him. I'm going to have to get Dani to show me how to tie that little knot. Since my lover enjoyed it so much I think we'll include some cock and ball torture in our play."

"I'm in," Mike announced, in a voice just shy of a whimper. *Ass*, he called himself for needing to struggle with his control.

"Are you, now? Do you know what you're signing up for?" Troy chuckled.

"Yes, damn it." Mike gritted his teeth and turned toward a smirking Troy. "You've made me keep my distance for too fucking long. She's mine, and I want her. Now."

Still grinning, Troy nodded, but didn't look in Mike's direction. "Well, you can't have her right now. Ransom and I tired her out from our play today. You can be Dani's toy tomorrow."

"Run, little man," Mike growled. "Fast and far."

Troy stood up and gave a languid stretch. "Yeah, yeah, I know, slow and painful."

CHAPTER 3

"Today we're going to use one of the smaller rooms on the main floor," Troy said as they strolled through the bar.

"Okay," Dani replied. "I'm excited, but nervous too."

"You have no reason to be nervous. You've learned well, and exude confidence in your position of Domme. You should be proud of what you've accomplished in the short time you've been practicing."

"Thank you, Troy. For everything."

"You are welcome." They came to a stop outside of one of the client rooms on the main floor of the club, and Troy reached for the door knob. "Now it's time for you to put practice into action. Keep in mind this is still considered training, therefore Ransom and I will be in the room with you. I have selected a submissive worthy of your talents, and he's waiting inside."

Dani's belly was fluttering with nervousness as she removed her coat and handed it to Troy. Today she wore a black corset with matching panties, fishnet stockings, and black, thigh-high leather boots.

Troy said nothing of the person he'd selected. Since she was still in training mode, she wondered if the chosen sub would merely be playing a role, or if this would be more real than with Ransom.

Ransom was a great sub in that he allowed her to use him to train with. He permitted her to paddle and flog him, advising her of pressure and technique. She'd enjoyed learning about all the erogenous zones on a man's body. Dani had no idea there were so many, or how sensitive they were. She was interested to see if she had the ability to stimulate a man's prostate gland.

The day before, Ransom had even been receptive to her trying out Japanese rope tying she'd read about, and let her lasso his boys. Yet, all along he had only been participating as a model, so to speak. With the help of the two lovers, she learned the Dominant's perspective through Troy, and a submissive's through Ransom. Now Dani was anxious to put all her practice into a real life Dominate-submissive situation. She was ready.

She also wondered if Troy would ease up on the rules from when she first started. What she wanted to do more than anything was sit down with Mike. Maybe go out with him sometime. Find out his likes and dislikes, and if he would consider choosing her as a Mistress.

After the session she was certain they would sit and discuss it like they always did, and decided that would be the time to bring up Mike. Who better to pump for a little info on the guy than his friends?

"I'm ready," she said.

With a nod, Troy turned the knob and pushed the door open.

Stepping into the room, Dani glanced around. Her eyes immediately settled on the submissive kneeling in the middle of the floor, and she stopped dead in her tracks. He was naked, his hands resting palms up on the tops of muscled thighs.

"Mike," she gasped softly, and watched as the semi-erect shaft between his legs came to life.

Troy's voice was behind her right ear. "You are his Mistress. You are in control."

"But you said a sub picks his Mistress. He didn't…"

"Yes, he has," Troy answered in a whisper, pointing to the firm flesh between Mike's legs. "Begin."

* * * *

Moments before, Mike had assumed the submissive position per Ransom's directions and waited patiently for her to come to him. His eyes were downcast, but as soon as the door opened the violet scent of her perfume assailed him. He fought the urge to lift his head to look at her.

If his cock got any harder it was going to explode. It felt as if hours were passing in silence, instead of seconds. What was she doing? What was she thinking? Was she disappointed to find him as her sub? He didn't think so. He'd seen the flicker of interest in her eyes whenever she saw him. Why the hell was it taking her so long to say something? As if reading his mind, the clicking of her heels announced her approach.

"On your feet," she said, coming to a stop in front of him. A slight waver was evident in her voice.

She was nervous.

Hell, so was he.

As he stood, Mike took in her attire and his aching balls threatened to unload. Passing her midsection, he caught the fragrance of her arousal, and his mouth watered. He fought the impulse to drag

[214]

his tongue along the crotch of her panties to sample her. The satin and lace covering her torso accentuated the fullness of her breasts, her narrow waist, and the sexy flair of her hips. What was supposed to be cups holding her boobs barely covered the pink of her areolas, and he was certain when he came up to his full height, he'd see nipple when he looked down. Mike suspected if he were to lay her out on the floor right now and start pounding himself into her, those puppies would bounce free in no time from the scrap of fabric covering them. He tried to keep his eyes lowered, knowing it was expected, but since he towered over her, even in those six-inch heels she wore, the attempt was futile.

Their eyes met.

The heat of desire simmered in the brown depths looking back at him. Mike was tempted to gather her in his arms and kiss her senseless.

"You're beautiful," he said.

Her left brow rose.

"My apologies, my Mistress, for speaking without permission," he offered to amend his error.

"Forgiven, *this* time," she replied. When she continued there was more confidence in her voice. "You have a safe word?"

It doesn't matter, baby, you won't be hearing it.

"Yes, my Mistress," he replied. "It's flower."

"You know when to use it?"

"Yes, Mistress."

Dani's eyes began to roam his body, and his flesh sizzled with every pass they took. After circling him once, she came to stand in front again. From between his thighs his cock stuck straight out, firm, proud, needing her touch. He was so fucking hard he was sure she could use his shaft like a tree branch and swing from it. When she reached out and placed her hands in the middle of his chest, a soft sigh left her lips.

"Your body is a work of art, slave," she whispered.

Mike stifled a groan as her fingers brushed over the puckered tips of his nipples.

"Thank you, Mistress."

He nearly winced when she squeezed the tight buds in warning, not from the slight pain she brought to them, but because of the jolt it sent to his already aching sac. The pads of her fingertips began exploring the bulges and ripples of muscle down the length of his arms before caressing back up and across his shoulders.

"I want you restrained," she announced

"Mmm, yes."

"And for that you will be punished."

It's about fucking time.

With a slender finger Dani pointed to the metal whipping post several feet away. Mike lowered his head and walked toward it. Eager to get his punishment under way, he fastened the restraints dangling from the top of the post around his wrists. The bindings were conveniently positioned for a sub to do up themselves.

"Good, slave," she praised, and ran her hands across his shoulders.

Her soft hands caressed the length of his back, and when she came to his ass, she cupped his cheeks. The tips of her fingers dug into his firm flesh, and he caught himself before the moan brewing slipped free. As her touch continued down his left leg, Mike's knees threatened to buckle.

"Spread your feet, slave."

He eagerly complied so she could fasten the strap around his ankle. Her hands repeated the same torture on his right leg. For a moment Mike thought about the picture he made, spread eagle and tied naked to a whipping post, with two of his buddies watching from the shadows. He didn't care about the audience. Hell, he and Dani could have been in the middle of the club for all to see, and it wouldn't have bothered him.

The woman of his dreams finally had her hands on him, and that was all that mattered.

"Should I use a paddle on you, slave, or a flogger?"

Use your bare hand, baby, just don't stop touching me.

"Mistress, I would be pleased with whichever you feel I deserve."

The clicking of her heels told him she was off to choose the implement for his punishment. He refused to lift his head to watch her walk away. His cock hadn't softened one iota, and he knew if he looked at her now, his tool would erupt like a geyser.

With a slow stride she closed the distance between them after choosing a weapon for pleasurable torture. He tensed as she pressed her body against his back. The heat of her full breasts touching the muscles of his back was like a firebrand on his flesh.

"I've decided you've earned a paddling for speaking without permission," she announced, and produced a length of polished wood for him to see.

"Thank you, my Mistress," Mike said.

"You will receive ten, and I want to hear you count them off."

"Yes, Mistress."

When the warmth of her body against his vanished, a chill caressed his heated skin. He shuddered as a tremor moved through him. Without any further warning, she struck him. The initial sting zipped through his nerve endings from the left cheek of his ass. Then the warmth of her hand soothed over the spot.

"One," he groaned.

The same attention was paid to his right cheek.

"Two."

Over and over the paddle made sweet contact with his ass. The delightful stinging made Mike's head spin like a top. Fire radiated from the taut globes, surging through his system. The ache in his balls was now beyond painful with the need for release. His cock throbbed in agony with every *thwack* of the wood against his burning ass.

"Yes, baby, yes," he heard himself mutter after the last swat.

Then she stopped. Over his shoulder he heard her harsh breath. "What did you say?" she asked in a raspy voice.

"Nothing, my Mistress," he lied, and then mentally kicked himself. If he'd kept talking without permission she would have continued.

As their session wore on Mike lost track of time. She tested her bondage techniques by restraining him on several pieces of equipment. When she took the flogger to him, Mike nearly passed out from pleasure. Troy and Ransom were correct, she was a natural with an implement.

Sweat coated his heated flesh, and his body ached. For what seemed like forever Mike teetered on the blissful edge between pleasure and pain. Both he could handle for a spell longer, but what he needed more than anything was to slide himself inside her. He wanted to feel her body welcoming him in, gripping and pulsing around his cock. He knew she was in a state no better than him. The scent of her arousal teased his nose. A sexy sheen of perspiration glistened on her skin.

When she hadn't touched him for what seemed like an eternity, he glanced down. Dani had dropped to her knees. Her breath was ragged, harsh, her breasts heaving. As she studied him, her body seemed to tremble. His eyes shifted to the object holding her attention. Between his legs his cock throbbed. The broad crown was an angry red, and droplets of pre-cum dribbled from the slit at the end.

Reaching for him, her hands gripped his hips. The tips of her fingers dug into his firm flesh. Then she leaned into him. Mike held his breath as she drew nearer to his aching shaft. Relief was in sight. It was as though she moved in slow motion, taunting him with that luscious mouth merely an inch away.

Yes, baby, just a little further. Please...

"That's enough for today." Troy's voice boomed in the room the moment Dani's lips parted.

A strangled croak erupted from Mike's throat, as a sound of frustration slipped from Dani's. Frustrated brown eyes glanced up at him. A flicker of defiance glinted in those eyes, and he suspected she was torn between finishing what she'd started and following the word of the Master.

Mike raised a brow, issuing her a silent challenge.

Dani shot a look over her shoulder toward Troy, and then back to Mike's groin. Her voice wavered with the trembling of her body. "But..." Dani said.

Troy lifted his chin, daring her to defy him. Tense moments passed in silence, as Mike watched helplessly while she struggled over what to do. If she defied Troy, she would be punished, that was the way. Mike didn't have a clue what her punishment would be, only that it would happen, and Troy would mete it out. As much as Mike enjoyed the thought of Dani's ass being paddled, he'd be damned if any other man would have the honor.

Dani dropped her gaze to the floor.

"Yes, Master," she replied, and her hands caressed down the length of Mike's legs to where his ankles were bound.

"Leave them," Troy said. "Ransom will untie him. Come."

Dani stood, and her legs wobbled beneath her.

Restrained to the metal pillory Mike could only watch as she staggered across the room to stand before Troy. After he wrapped an oversized bathrobe around her trembling body, he escorted her to the door, and out of the room.

"He's a dead man," Mike growled as Ransom approached and knelt to undo the straps around his ankles.

Ransom remained quiet as he reached to release the buckle around

Mike's right wrist, and then the left. Taking a few minutes to stretch his muscles, Mike grumbled under his breath. Beside the apparatus hung a towel, he grabbed it and unceremoniously dragged it over his body, drying the layer of sweat shining on his heated skin.

"He left you in a bad way, pal," Ransom said, a hint of amusement in his voice. "That wasn't right."

"The son of bitch will pay." Mike stomped across the floor to the chair in the corner where he'd left his clothes.

There was no way in hell the boner he currently sported would be going away any time soon. The nerve of Troy stopping them when Dani was so obviously interested in taking things further; and Mike was more than happy to let her. After tugging on his baggy sweat pants and attempting to adjust the noticeable protrusion in the front, Mike flung the door open and stormed out.

His big, aroused body lumbered up the hall, every step more agonizing than the last. No amount of pulling was going to alleviate the present state of his cock. The only thing that would bring him relief would be to lose himself in Dani's body, but with Troy continuing to torture him, that was likely never to happen.

"Watch out!" Ransom hollered from behind him. "Big man coming through."

He could picture the smug smirk that he knew was curling his friend's lips. Over his shoulder Mike scowled at Ransom and walked with purpose through the bar area. He was certain steam was shooting out his ears, he was so frustrated. The nerve of Troy cutting their session off before either of them found release.

"What's up with him?" Deirdre asked wide-eyed.

"Blue balls."

"Ahh, the poor guy," she replied with sympathy. "Dani give his boys a hard time?"

Ransom shook his head, still grinning. "Troy put a stop to their session before they..." He stopped and chuckled. "You know."

Deirdre burst out in laughter. "Christ, he is cruel, isn't he? Poor Mike."

From behind the bar Mike grabbed a liter bottle of water before stomping toward the back door leading to the private suites and the gym area. No amount of running—regardless of the distance—was going to make him feel better, but it was worth a try.

* * * *

Upstairs in Troy and Ransom's suite, Dani stood under the heated downpour of their shower. Troy had insisted she relax after the session before getting behind the wheel of her car. Appreciating his sentiment, Dani agreed. When they'd arrived upstairs she realized the encounter had been tougher on her than she thought it would be. Perhaps it had something to do with the man in the position as her submissive.

The minute she'd stepped into the playroom her body reacted. The dampness between her legs when Mike was around was something she'd become somewhat accustomed to. Somewhat. However, when she spotted his naked body kneeling on the floor, she found herself on the brink of orgasm. The swelling of her breasts made her wonder if they were going to leap right out of the bustier she'd been wearing, in offering. The tightening of her nipples had sent a sharp spasm south to the painful throbbing of her clit.

The harder they'd played, the harder they'd both sweated. Rivulets of salty liquid had run freely over their bodies.

As Dani showered, images of Mike strapped to the St. Andrew's cross played in her mind. It had been all she could do to stop herself from lapping up the perspiration that trickled all over his bulging flesh. The twitching of his muscles had danced in time to the quivering of her belly. Despite the dim lighting in the playroom, his damp skin was flushed. Pink tinted his cheeks, and his eyes gleamed with excitement when they met hers.

She'd never been more turned on in her life. Shivers had coursed through her body each and every time he cast a glance her way. The nightly dreams she had of Mike's hands gripping her hips, slamming into her from behind—after he'd earned it, of course—tormented her wakened state as well.

The broad expanse of his chest as he drew deep labored breaths made her reach out to stroke the firm swells of his pecs, to soak up the heat of desire emanating from his body. Beneath her fingertips, his muscles had twitched. Tight, brown nipples protruded and darkened as his need escalated.

With a washcloth lathered up, she began dragging it across her fevered skin. Instead of feeling relieved at washing the sweat from her body, her arousal soared once again.

Despite everything she'd learned over the weeks Dani hadn't been able to reel in her own desire, and she had dropped to her knees in front of Mike. Her hands had caressed the length of his powerful, toned legs with firm pressure, needing to feel every ripple and divot of the taut flesh making up his limbs.

Dropping the washcloth to the floor, Dani ran her soapy hands over her body, her mind racing with thoughts of Mike.

While on the floor she'd found herself facing the most delicious looking length of cock she'd ever laid eyes on. The fat crown at the end was swollen, a deep purple color, and leaking with mouth-watering droplets of pre-cum.

She'd never needed to taste anything as badly in her life.

Mike's erection had looked both painful and inviting as it bobbed before her. Knowing she wouldn't be able to fit the whole thing in her mouth, she was prepared to gag herself silly just to sample him. She needed him on her tongue. Filling her mouth. Unloading himself inside her.

Leaning forward she'd parted her lips to taste her fill, and then... Without warning, or any reason for doing so other than to be a dick, Troy stopped her. The rotten son of a...

"That's enough for today," she mocked in the steam swirling around her. "The nerve."

For the moment Dani opted not to give in to the desire to bring herself to orgasm. Oh no. She decided that on her way home she was going to stop by the adult store around the corner from her apartment to purchase a new dildo that resembled the size and shape of Mike's cock. If she wasn't going to be permitted the real thing, for now she'd have to settle for an imitation. The situation bit, no question, but she'd make do. For now.

Reaching down to turn off the water, she slid the glass door to one side and stepped out onto the bathmat. A knock sounded at the closed door as she wrapped one towel around her hair and another around her body.

"Come in. It's open."

The door swung open, and Troy took a couple of steps inside. "I've brought you something to put on." He held out a pair of sweat pants and a t-shirt. "I thought these might be more comfortable than the lingerie you had on earlier."

Glancing up, she met his gaze and narrowed her eyes. "Why did you stop me?"

"Control. You were about to lose it."

"No, I wasn't," she argued, snatching the clothes from his outstretched hand. "I just wanted to...to..."

Troy leaned against the doorframe and grinned. Tugging the t-shirt over her head, she dropped the towel to the floor, stepped into the fleece pants, and pulled the drawstring tight. Both were miles too big for her. Unwinding the towel around her head, she began vigorously rubbing at the damp locks.

Damn right she'd been about to lose it, but she didn't want to appear weak and admit that. She glanced over at Troy, who was still grinning, watching her, a knowing glint sparkling in his gray eyes.

"I'm not Domme material," she admitted with sadness.

"No, not entirely," he responded in agreement, and pushed himself away from the frame. Approaching from behind her as she stood in front of the vanity mirror, Troy reached for the towel and took

[225]

over drying her hair. "What is it you were looking for when you came to me a month ago?"

"I wanted to be in control."

"Of what, specifically?"

"Of my sex life."

"Okay. How so?"

"My sex life has never been fulfilling. Hell, I even let myself down sometimes." A nervous giggle slipped past her lips, but Troy simply nodded. "My past lovers have always been in such a hurry to race to the finish line, I'm left to tend to my own needs. It's my own fault though."

"In what way?"

Troy tossed the wet towel on the vanity, and wrapped his arms around her in a friendly embrace. They still stood staring back at one another in the mirror.

"I've allowed the man to take the lead, expecting him to know what I want and what I need. And in doing so, I've learned that men don't know jack-shit about how to please a woman."

Troy laughed. "True, some don't, and some don't care to know. But there are men out there who do, and want to. And if they don't know how, they're willing to learn."

"That's all well and good, but this whole time I've been concentrating on how to make my submissive feel good. What's been in it for me?"

Troy quirked a half-smile and tightened his arms around her. "Think about it, kid. What was different about today than every day you've spent with Ransom?"

Dani began to mentally replay the couple of hours she'd spent with Mike.

"Think it aloud," Troy said. "I want to hear it."

"First off, Mike had an erection," she replied. "The whole time. The poor guy looked so pained."

"He'll get over it," Troy said with a wink.

Dani gave him an elbow to the ribs. "That wasn't nice leaving him in that condition."

"No, it wasn't. I admit it. Don't worry, he's already planning his revenge on me, I assure you."

"What do you mean?"

"In case you haven't realized it, Mike finds you incredibly attractive, and has been making my life hell since you came in that first day."

Dani's eyes widened as she looked at Troy's reflection. "R-really?"

"Yes, he's threatened to kill me, slowly—"

"No, not that. Hell, I'm seriously thinking about killing you after today," she said. "He thinks I'm attractive?"

"You saw the boner he was sporting. It was all for you."

Dani stood silent, excited to learn that Mike was interested in her.

"Come on, you've seen the way he looks at you. Have your past experiences been that abysmal? Has no one ever looked at you with hunger?"

She shook her head. "I can't honestly say that anyone has."

"That's a real shame, because you are a beautiful woman, Dani."

"Thanks," she said and dropped her gaze.

"Okay, back to what it is you seek in being a Domme."

"Control."

"Expand on that."

"In coming here I'd hoped to learn how to be in control of my own sexuality. In doing so, I'd be more apt to ask my lover to do things that bring me pleasure. I want to experiment, try new things. The idea of bondage thrills me. I've never been restrained, except when you and Ransom were showing me, but never while playing with a lover. I don't know if I'd like to be tied up, but I liked being in control. Setting the pace, possessing power over the situation, not necessarily my partner. Maybe it's because I don't feel like I have much control with my life in general." Dani blew out a breath in a huff.

Troy remained silent, his eyes encouraging her to continue.

"That came out wrong. I have friends I adore, and would do anything for—by the way, you and Ransom rank right up there, too…"

Troy's right eye winked.

"I love working with my parents, and my customers are terrific. I'm stuck in a sexual rut, and I'm tired of going at it single handed. But I guess I'm just not cut out to be a dominatrix."

"Who says you're not?"

"Well, I do. I think I'm even more confused than I was in the beginning. The training has been helpful, but I need to see if I've got what it takes, for real. In a real setting without you and Ransom to back me up."

"We didn't interfere today."

Dani cocked a brow. "Oh, really?"

Troy ignored her. "Listen to me. Some people want, or in some circumstances need to be in control one hundred percent of the time. Some folks have what it takes to remain in control of their emotions and desires, all of the time. Others do not, and there is nothing wrong with it, either way. People do what they are comfortable with, or at least they should.

"You want to explore your sexuality, and you should embrace that. You want more than a vanilla experience, to try new things. Sex is supposed to be fun, Dani, and if you aren't having fun, you're not doing it right. I think it's terrific you want to explore what's out there. More people should do that. If people were less sexually repressed the world would be a better place.

"Believe me, for you, sweetheart, with the right person you will find you gain pleasure and complete satisfaction in either position. You have what it takes to be in control, but you also possess a desire to submit, to be pushed beyond your limits. The right man will make you see stars. All you have to do is reach out and seize the opportunity."

"I was just about to do that when you stopped me."

"Get over it. I stopped your fun, because next time—"

Dani spun around in Troy's arms and smiled up at him. "Next time?"

"It'll be worth the wait." He pressed a friendly kiss to her forehead. "Control, Mistress Dani. Oh, and I heard you muttering something about a giant dildo while you were showering. Don't bother.

There's no substitute for the real thing."

Taking a step back, she glared at Troy. "You and Mike?"

Throwing his head back, Troy laughed. "No. Mike's a great guy, but not my type. He's hetero, with no interest in trying out the other side."

Dani sighed with relief. She wouldn't have been put off if Mike was bi, but she found herself wanting to be the sole focus of his attention, if the opportunity presented itself.

And she intended there to be an opportunity.

Dani stepped out of Troy's arms, turned back to the mirror, and finger combed her hair. "I've got to go," she said. "My body is still on fire after the session, and if I don't get myself to the diner I'm going to stop by the naughty store to pick me up a new toy, and call in sick."

Troy chuckled, placing his hand against her back as they walked toward the door. "Savor the anticipation," he said. "The next time—"

"Yeah, you already said that. You think—"

"There'll be no stopping it. Listen, Ransom and I have been talking, and if your friend is interested, we'd like to meet her."

"Cool. But I don't want her to feel like it's a set up. I was hoping the encounter could be more spontaneous. You know, like maybe we'd come here together, and nature could just take its course?"

"We will not force her," Troy said.

"No, of course not. Forcing is wrong. But if she were to 'cross the threshold'..."

"You are a very sneaky girl, Dani."

"Yes, I can be," she agreed with a grin. "Meg's got some

baggage," she continued as they left the suite.

"A lover?"

"Nothing like that. She hasn't been involved with anyone for years. Gave up on dating long ago. Her baggage is her dad. He's the senator who lobbied tooth and nail to stop this place from opening."

"Hmm, interesting."

"What's that supposed to mean?" she asked over her shoulder. "Meg's not like her parents."

"I meant nothing at all, Dani. Just thinking aloud. How about we arrange something for Friday night?"

"Okay. I'll see what I can do."

At the bottom of the stairs Troy opened the door to the bar area.

"I need to use the little girls' room. I should have gone before I left your suite. I'll see myself out," she said.

"All right. Take care and we'll see you tomorrow," Troy said.

"Goodbye."

Dani strolled toward the corridor leading to the restrooms. After relieving herself she started to cross the bar to leave when Mike entered through a door marked *PRIVATE*, stopping in her tracks. His chest was bare, and sweat glistened on his torso. Though he attempted to dry himself with a towel, the delicious rivulets of his spent energies trickled freely.

Warmth in her lower belly became hot, burning as it traveled south toward the clenching between her legs. A second later the crotch of her borrowed sweat pants dampened. She felt herself inching forward, prepared to throw herself at his feet and beg him to take her right then and there, but a feral glint in his eyes froze her in place. Chills ricocheted throughout her body as her arousal gained momentum. This was what Troy was talking about. It's all about being with the right man. At the moment Dani wanted to dominate him until she had her fill, and then submit to his wants and needs.

"Sorry about my appearance." The deep smokiness in Mike's voice made her nipples harden even more. "I've been working off my frustration in the gym."

"I feel terrible you were left so uncomfortable," she said, her voice shaky. "I wasn't much better."

Mike cocked a brow in her direction.

"I'm told it will heighten our anticipation for next time," she added.

The front of Mike's pants began to come to life. Dani felt a surge of confidence. She stepped forward until she was standing a couple of inches from him. The musky scent of him after working out made her knees weak. The sight of his muscles twitching under her gaze made her toes curl. The heat radiating from his body seeped into her despite the short distance separating them. Mike's breath was shallow as he attempted to control it. A thick vein in his neck pulsed in time to the throbbing between her thighs.

"Friday night," Dani said hoarsely, and bent her weak knees.

When her face was aligned with his mid-abdomen, she stuck out her tongue and leaned forward. Dipping the tip into the indent of Mike's belly button, she began to rise slowly, pressing the flat of her tongue against him. Up the center of his body she traveled, savoring the salty taste of his flesh and the trembling of his big frame. On her tiptoes, she stretched to catch a trickle of sweat racing down the divot below his Adam's apple.

Though feeling far from sated, she took a step backward and licked her lips. Fire burned in Mike's brown eyes as he stared at her. At the sides of his muscled physique his right hand gripped the towel he'd been using to sop up perspiration, and in the left he'd crushed an empty plastic water bottle.

"Friday night, nothing will stop me from finishing what I start with you." The promise was clear in her steady voice. She fought the urge to cheer in triumph when a grin began to curl his full lips.

"Until then, my Mistress," was all he said.

Dani stepped around his frame, and walked through the front door. Once outside on the sidewalk, she drew a deep breath and held it. After exhaling, she pulled in another and released it slowly. As she was about to open her car door, someone called her name.

"Miss Miller."

Dani turned to find a man jogging toward her. As he drew near, she recognized him from her friend Natalie's work place. Max Renfrew. Natalie had a huge crush on the man and talked about him nonstop. Dani didn't understand why Nat just didn't tell him how she felt. But then, she herself seemed to lack the nerve to tell Mike she was hot for him.

"I'm sorry to bother you, but I was hoping to catch you before you left today," he said, drawing to a stop before her. "I'm Max Renfrew."

"I know who you are. You work with my friend Natalie at the magazine. I've seen you many times when I've gone to meet Nat for lunch."

Max looked a mite taken aback, and then grinned. "Has she, uh, ever mentioned me?"

"Only all the time," Dani said, and then bit her tongue. "I really shouldn't have said that. Just strike that from your memory, would you? Please?"

Max shook his head. "Not a chance. I'd like to ask your help with something."

* * * *

After Dani left the club, Mike stared absently at the closed door, replaying what she'd said. Friday she was going to make him her sex slave, and nothing was going to stop her. Fifty-two hours seemed like an eternity. How in the hell was he supposed to wait that long, and remain sane?

Mike glanced at the clock on the wall behind the bar. Fifty-one hours, fifty-eight minutes to go. He was going to die from the sheer torture of it all. A throat clearing behind him cut into his thoughts. He turned to find a grinning Troy watching him.

"You're welcome," Troy said.

"I could kiss you," Mike replied.

"Oh, I don't know, it was sort of fun around here when you wanted to kill me."

"Like right on the lips, I could kiss you," Mike added.

"The hell you can." Ransom chuckled as he walked in on their exchange. "Well, wait a minute, maybe you can. What did he do?"

"Presented the big man with a golden opportunity," Troy said. "To have his lust slaked by a curvy little brunette."

"You do owe him for the stunt you pulled this afternoon," Ransom said. "Poor guy. I watched him kick the shit out of the heavy bag in the weight room for an hour nonstop, chanting your name over and over. I thought you were a goner."

"Yeah, that was kinda' cruel. Water under the bridge now, right Mike?"

Mike chuckled and shook his head.

"So what's your plan then?" Troy asked.

"Dani seems to like me strapped to something, and you aren't going to catch me complaining. So I think I'll move the portable St. Andrew's cross up to my suite. The one with the Velcro restraints."

"I'll give you a hand," Ransom said.

"Thanks. If this works out like I'm hoping it will, I'm going to have to set up a playroom like you guys have. But I'll be damned if I'm going to be the one tied up all the time."

"Yeah? You see Dani bound and gagged?" Ransom asked, and then chuckled.

"Bound to a spanking horse, yes. Or maybe a bondage chair, spread eagle for my enjoyment. Gagged, no way. I want to hear her screaming my name. Hey Troy, do you think you could call your guy and order that paddle she wields so well? The damn thing stings like a bitch on contact, but I'd like to give my girl her very own."

"Already done," Troy replied.

* * * *

"Hey, anybody around here going to take my order?"

Being near closing time the only occupants in the diner were a couple of regulars, so the suddenness of a familiar voice caught Dani by surprise. She blinked herself back to the present and turned toward the sound of the voice that had interrupted her x-rated daydream of Mike.

"There you are."

"Hi, Meg. Sorry, I guess I was—"

"As usual you're staring off into space with your head in the clouds."

"Yeah, something like that. What are you having, girlfriend?"

"Coffee, strong, along with something gooey and fattening. Did your mom make any pies today? Like maybe her award winning apple caramel?"

"You know it. A day my mom doesn't make a pie, is a day the sun doesn't come up." Dani disappeared into the back.

When she returned, Megan had poured two cups of coffee. Dani cut generous slices of pie, and served Meg one.

"Mom tried something different with the crust to make it less fattening."

"But I want fattening," Megan whined, then laughed.

"Well, she didn't skimp on the caramel. Dig in," she said, handing her friend a fork.

Both girls slid a forkful of pie into their mouths, and sighed in utter contentment.

"This is good," Megan moaned.

"Mom switched the apples up."

"Nat called this afternoon to say she's off this weekend," Megan said, clearing the last bite of flaky crust from her plate.

Max had mentioned earlier that Natalie would be off. He arranged it with their boss, so as to set his plan into motion.

"So I was thinking the three of us should paint the town red. It's been weeks since we did something together, and I'm missing you guys. What do you think?" Meg asked.

"Sound great. What do you have in mind?" Dani asked, collecting their empty plates.

"I thought maybe you might want to pick what we do. Nat said she didn't care, and I always choose."

"That's because you always have great ideas," Dani said. "But okay, I'm up for the challenge of deciding on the night's entertainment. Let's see... How about Friday night at Le Club d'Esclavage?"

"The BDSM nightclub?" Megan's tone carried curiosity, despite the fact she looked at Dani with wide owl eyes.

"Sure. Why not?"

Megan bit her lower lip, seeming to consider Dani's suggestion. A moment later she shrugged. "Why not, indeed. I'm sort of curious to get a glimpse inside, since my dad fought so hard against its opening. And the article Nat's magazine did on it was kind of intriguing. Wasn't it?"

"Oh, yeah," Dani said in agreement. "Definitely."

"We'll need reservations or something, won't we?"

"Leave it to me. We only need a reservation for the private playrooms, but if we don't want to be waiting in line all night we'll want our names on the guest list."

Megan raised a questioning brow in Dani's direction.

"So I've heard," she quickly added. Friday night her friends would get a glimpse into her secret life. "I'll take care of the details."

Megan sat and kept Dani company until closing time. At eight o'clock Dani locked up for the night, and then invited her friend back to her apartment to continue their visit. Popping a cork from a bottle of Chablis, the two sat out on the balcony enjoying the cool evening air.

Dani was excited that Megan had suggested she pick the locale for their evening out. Since speaking with Max earlier she wasn't sure how to broach the subject of spending Friday evening at Le Club d'Esclavage with her friends. With Meg on board all they had to do was convince Natalie.

The two friends decided to keep their Friday night plans a secret from Natalie, until just the right moment. If Natalie knew they were planning on taking her to the hottest BDSM club within a hundred mile radius, she'd freak. She wasn't a prude. Nat just despised the club scene all the way around. After learning that the object of Natalie's fantasies was of similar mind where her interests were concerned, Dani didn't feel the least bit bad dragging her friend into the nightclub. She suspected once they were inside, and Max made his presence known, Nat would relax and have a good time.

Then there was Megan. Perhaps it was her dominant side that helped Dani to recognize her friend's submissive nature. Before meeting Troy and Ransom, and experimenting herself, Dani hadn't been certain what to call it. Now she knew. It excited her that Troy had agreed to meet Meg, and if she were willing, he and Ransom would show her the pleasures to be enjoyed at the hands of a man, or men, who knew how to push her beyond her comfort zone.

Dani knew the rules regarding play at the club, inside and out. Nothing would happen if all parties were not in complete agreement on the terms. Forced play was never tolerated within the premises of the club. Her friends would be in very good hands.

But what about her? Would she be in good hands?

What did she know of Mike? Not a hell of a lot. In fact, nothing. She now knew he thought her attractive, and found enjoyment in the brief playtime they'd been given.

The desire and hunger in his eyes when he looked at her made her pulse race. Not once in her past had a look alone sent her body soaring toward climax. With just a glance he set her body on fire. Never in a million years would she have thought it even possible, if she wasn't experiencing it for herself.

Dani's anticipation level shot through the roof. She'd made a decision after leaving the club and Mike earlier, that to build the keenness for the both of them, despite wanting to, she wasn't going to go back to the club until Friday night.

This was going to be the longest couple of days of her life.

CHAPTER 4

Mike glanced around the spare bedroom in his suite, which up until now had been empty, and smiled. With Ransom and Troy's help, he'd turned the twenty feet by fifteen feet space into a sexual playground.

Several pieces of bondage equipment, all portable, were placed around the room. A St. Andrew's cross, which Dani seemed to enjoy so much, sat kitty-corner along the far wall. In the middle of the room a bondage chair had been erected, complete with leather buckled restraints and adjustable back. The seat was split, so when he shackled Dani to it, she'd be completely exposed for him. Off to one side Mike placed a wooden spanking bench, padded for a sub's comfort. It didn't matter to him if tonight it went unused, visually it added to the ambience of the setup.

A variety of tables, different heights, had been brought in, and the tops of them were decorated with pillar candles, bottles of lubes, and a dozen or so toys. Floggers and paddles were hung on one wall, mirrors placed on the others. By the time the men were finished, Mike's spare room had been turned into a suitable dungeon for pleasurable torture.

There was an agonizing twenty-four hours to go.

* * * *

Friday morning arrived and Dani was stoked. She'd barely slept a wink and was running full tilt on adrenaline. Nothing was going to bring her down today. After pulling the morning shift at her parents' diner, she raced home to spend the afternoon primping for the evening.

With the surface of her bed covered in lingerie it took over an hour for Dani to narrow her choices of attire down to six skimpy outfits—or rather scraps of silk and lace, and leather.

"Now with my undies taken care of, let's find something to wear over them," she said to the fat cat curled up by the pillows.

She searched her closet and decided on a red leather miniskirt with a black silk shell style tank top. Beneath the snug-fitting leather she opted for black lace thong panties and a matching demi-cup bra. The bra pushed her boobs up and out as more of an offering than for support.

"Perfect," she purred, examining her reflection in the mirror.

Right on time a cab pulled up in front of Dani's apartment with Megan in the rear seat. Together they rode over to Natalie's. On the drive to the club, Dani and Megan chatted while Natalie, seated between them, gazed out the window, paying them no attention.

"Okay, Meg," Natalie said, breaking into their conversation. "Where are you taking me?" Her expression was one of annoyance.

The two women giggled, and then Dani grabbed Natalie's hand and kissed the back of it. Her friend looked so stressed out. "Nat, you really need to take a load off. You're going to get all wrinkly before you're thirty if you don't let go of all that stress."

"Dani's right, Nat. Now that the Marsden project is finished and on its way to print, it's time you let those gorgeous curls down and cut loose! Hell, we haven't spent any time with you since you were assigned that account. So tonight, you are ours."

"Well, for a little while anyway." Dani wagged her brows.

"What the hell is that suppose to mean? Oh God, what are you two up to?" Natalie asked. Her apprehension was evident in her voice.

They just smiled mysteriously.

Five minutes later the taxi rolled to a stop.

"*Oooh* we're here!" Megan and Dani squealed in unison.

After Megan paid the driver, they stepped out of the car. Dani attempted to stifle a snicker at the stunned expression on Natalie's face.

"Oh...my...God," Natalie gasped. "We are not going in there." She shook her head as she gaped at Dani and Megan.

"Damn straight," Megan replied. She and Dani linked their arms with Natalie and headed for the front door, bypassing those waiting in line.

As they approached, Dani spotted Mike, and nearly creamed her panties. He wore a black suit, with a red silk dress shirt under the jacket. The color matched her miniskirt. The waves of his dark hair had been neatly tamed, and the seduction-laced smile he flashed her threatened to buckle her knees. His brown eyes flared with desire, and arousal. The glimmer of curiosity sparkling in their depths made her belly flutter.

Tonight was going to be fun. She was going to take control and rein in the man who'd been tormenting her sleep for the past month.

[243]

Then maybe, just maybe, she'd relinquish some of that control, and give him the opportunity to tame her.

"Hi, Mikey." Dani tipped her head coyly, greeting him as he reached for the door handle.

A couple of times Dani overheard Deirdre call him Mikey, and instantly fell in love with how easily it made him blush. His slight embarrassment at her using the name didn't disappoint. The flash of color happened so quickly, she was certain no one but her saw it.

"Good evening, ladies. Welcome to Le Club d'Esclavage," he said, and then winked at Dani.

Natalie spun her head around to gap at Dani, a shocked look on her face. "Dani, have you—"

"Maybe once or twice." Dani couldn't contain her snickering this time. "Now come on. Let's get in there."

Dani pulled them through the door Mike held open, and as she sashayed past him, he stopped her. "I'll meet you in there shortly." His suggestive smile sent her pulse racing. An eager giggle slipped out her mouth as she followed her two friends inside.

Inside the club the music was loud and infectious. The vast open area pulsed with energy. The people on the dance floor moved as one in time to the throbbing bass.

Several of her training sessions occurred during the club's regular business hours, so Dani wasn't the least bit surprised by the state of dress—or rather undress—of the club's clientele. The majority of the patrons on the dance floor and mingling around the bar were scarcely dressed, in barely-there leather straps wrapping this way and that.

Women wore bustiers that pushed their naked breasts up and out for everyone's viewing pleasure. Many of the men wore leather pants with the backside missing, showing off ass cheeks of all sizes, or some type of pouch encasing their genitals.

Sweaty bodies bumped and grinded against one another on the dance floor. Couples of every variety—males with females, males with males, females with females, and a few threesomes—kissed, stroked and rubbed each other as they swayed to the music.

Dani glanced at her two friends who wore matching expressions of astonishment.

The night is young, ladies, she thought. *Just wait and see what's in store for you.*

After a few minutes of silence, a look of acceptance crossed Megan's face, and her shoulders relaxed.

Good sign.

A familiar song filled the room, and Megan began to move in time to the beat. She leaned between Natalie and Dani and said, "This is awesome."

Now to get Nat to let loose.

"I told you so." Dani giggled and started dancing with Megan as the trio made their way toward the bar.

For the next hour the girls danced and chit-chatted. Dani was immensely pleased that her friends now seemed to be enjoying the atmosphere of the club. Natalie sat on a barstool and rocked back and forth to the music.

A half hour earlier Dani had spotted Max watching them from the other side of the bar where the lights were much dimmer. Ransom was also in place. Neither man would approach the trio. The plan was for Dani and Mike to venture off first. Ransom would then gain Megan's attention, luring her away from Natalie. Once Nat was alone, Max would make his move. As if on cue, with their backs turned toward the dance floor, a huge shadow blocked out the flashing lights.

Mike.

Fighting the urge to turn around and throw herself at him, Dani took a deep breath and attempted to get her raging hormones in check. As they spun around to face him, Dani put her game face on. It was beyond difficult to maintain her Domme persona when she met the heated look of a predator in his eyes. His six-five frame towered over her. That was something she loved about him. Just his presence made her feel safe, protected.

"Are you finished for the night?" she asked evenly, her tone a complete opposite to the flirtatious one she used with him when they entered the club earlier.

"I'm all yours, my Mistress," he replied.

Without a word she reached up, grabbed the silk tie dangling from his neck, and gave a light tug. "Enjoy your evening, ladies," she heard him say to Megan and Natalie as he followed behind.

As they strolled through the gyrating, sweaty bodies on the dance floor, Dani slowed, realizing she hadn't reserved a room for the night's activities. She couldn't take Mike to Troy and Ransom's suite. If things went according to plan, the two of them would have Megan up there in short order.

Seeming to sense her sudden hesitation, Mike came through. "Take the stairs," he said close to her ear.

The bouncer at the top allowed them to pass, and from behind Mike urged her to continue down the darkened corridor. When they came to a closed door at the end, he reached around her, slid a key into the deadbolt lock, and gave a flick of his wrist.

"Turn the knob," he instructed.

The warmth of his breath wafted across her cheek. She did, and they entered the passage. After locking the deadbolt behind them, Mike placed the palm of his hand against the small of her back, proceeding forward.

"At the end of the hall, turn to the right."

When they reached their destination Mike slid a key into another lock.

"This is my personal suite," he stated, barely above a whisper, and pushed the door open.

Dani stared straight ahead, silent. This was her moment of truth.

"Are you ready to tame my beast?" he asked.

A chill of arousal snaked its way throughout her body. Dani felt her confidence grow tenfold. "Yes," she answered and stepped inside.

"Then allow me to show you what I've prepared over the past couple of days."

"All right."

The heat of Mike's hand pressing against the small of her back radiated throughout her body. As they strolled through the apartment, she glanced around. Simple furnishing served a purpose of practicality rather than flare. A worn floral patterned sofa stretched across the longest wall. A recliner held together with strips of duct tape sat in front of a moderately-sized television. Mike's suite was cozy, comfortable. Homey. A place she could see herself living quite happily.

Numerous pictures hung unevenly on the walls around the living room, the subjects smiling, enjoying each other. Dani spotted Mike in several, standing with who she assumed were his family.

"You have a lovely family," she said.

"Thank you. We're very close."

"Where are you in the pecking order?" she asked, noting a couple of portraits of studio quality.

"Youngest. My sisters are twins and seven years older than me. How about you?"

A tinge of envy panged her. How nice it would have been to be raised with siblings. "Only child. But have great friends."

"Here we are."

Mike encouraged her to round the corner and enter the room. The breath caught in Dani's chest as the room illuminated dimly before them. Her gaze darted around the room, taking in the smaller scale version of Troy and Ransom's playroom. Mike's was more intimate.

"This is perfect," she said, glancing up at him after taking a visual inventory of the supplies and decor.

"You like?"

"I love. Now," she said, stepping into the room and dropping her purse behind the door. With a turn she met his heated gaze, and her belly somersaulted. Crooking her finger, she motioned him forward.

"Get in here, and get those clothes off."

"Very well, my Mistress."

Mike entered, slipping his suit jacket off. He folded it neatly and placed it over the back of a chair beside the door, followed by his tie. With their gazes locked, his blunt fingertips slid buttons through button holes, then worked the dress shirt over broad shoulders. The same attention to folding was paid to the shirt. His chest muscles rippled, calling out for her touch.

Dani ran her tongue across her lower lip as Mike reached for his pants. As he kicked off his loafers he pushed the thick leather of his belt past the brass buckle, and pulled it through the loops. He laid it on top of the dress shirt. A deft flick released the fastening of his pants. Then he lowered the zipper. Slowly. Teasing. Over his hips, down powerful legs, he pushed the fabric to the floor, along with his underwear. Mike bent over to retrieve the discarded pants. Before standing he tugged off his socks, tossing them under the chair with his shoes. He folded the pants, laying them on the seat of the chair.

Dani blew out a sigh of appreciation. He was stunning.

"Now your turn," he said in a smoky voice.

She cocked her head. "I'm in charge here."

"Of course, my Mistress." He grinned wickedly. "I thought you would be more comfortable without so many clothes on. I suspect we'll be working up quite a sweat."

No doubt!

"At least that's my hope," he added.

For a moment she pondered his suggestion. How thoughtful of

him to express concern for her comfort. And since Mike had shed his clothing, the temperature seemed to have shot up numerous degrees.

"You're right," she said.

Dani gripped the hem of her shirt with shaky hands and slowly tugged the fabric up and over her head. When Mike held his hand out for the garment, she passed it to him. She watched as he folded the shirt, then placed it atop his pile of discarded attire. Once again his gaze, so full of lust, settled on her. A single nod, her cue to continue.

She reached behind her back for the fastening of her skirt. After releasing the closure she pushed the leather over the flare of her hips and stepped out. Mike held out his hand for the skirt. Dani knelt to retrieve it from the floor, then stood and handed it over. Again, he folded her piece of clothing before setting it aside. Clothed in her bra and panties she went back to admiring his nakedness.

Now that it was just the two of them, Dani's anxieties were niggling. From the moment she laid eyes on Mike she'd wanted to be with him. It was insane the attraction she felt toward him since she knew nothing about him. The physical attraction between them was undeniable as she watched his cock harden and lengthen before her eyes. If she had a penis it would probably look the same way. She didn't think she'd ever been as aroused as she was at the moment. She couldn't help but wonder if there could be something more between them than just this one night.

The craving to explore his big, muscled body with her hands grew to overwhelming proportions. She needed like she'd never needed before. She needed to possess him, and to have him possess her as well.

Moisture threatened to explode from her core. Her nipples distended painfully as his eyes roamed from her face down to her toes. The slow path they traveled made her flesh goose pimple. When he began an upward sweep with his visual caress her knees threatened to buckle.

"I have a present for you." The sound of his voice brought her out of the erotic daydream. Breaking their gaze, Mike crossed the floor to a small table standing beside a wooden whipping post.

Turning on his heel, he closed the distance separating them and presented her a polished wooden paddle like the one she'd used on him a couple of days before. "I would be honored for you to use this on me, my Mistress."

As if suddenly remembering she was the one in charge, Dani summoned her control and took the paddle from Mike's outstretched hands.

"Very well, slave. Turn around and grip the handles of that whipping post."

A glimmer of arousal flickered in Mike's eyes. A grin tugged at the corner of his mouth. Dani's pulse raced.

"I won't restrain you. But don't even think of letting go of those grips," she warned.

"As you wish, Mistress."

Mike turned and reached for the handles on either side of the apparatus. His long, thick fingers wrapping around the rubber grips made Dani fantasize about his hands on her body. Without being told he spread his feet slightly wider than the distance of his broad shoulders.

Dani approached the naked man who'd taunted her dreams for weeks. Though she'd enjoyed their session together a couple of days earlier, she aimed to ensure their time tonight would be something neither of them would soon forget. In fact, if she played her cards right there would be plenty of nights like this.

"Before the other day had you ever been paddled?" she asked.

Each of them had a past. Nothing could change that, and Dani wasn't jealous of the past women in Mike's life. What mattered was the woman he may have after this night. The curiosity behind her question was simply to determine if he practiced the lifestyle full-time, or if he just dabbled.

Unable to resist any longer Dani reached out to stroke her hand across his shoulders. The muscles danced under her tentative touch. Though the bulges were firm, tight, his skin was soft.

"Yes," he replied.

"And you enjoyed it?"

"Not nearly as much as when you are the one wielding the implement, Mistress."

Good answer, she mused.

Down his back her hands caressed, lower until she reached the taut cheeks of his ass. She would have loved to bend over and sink her teeth into first one globe, then the other, but the man had asked for a paddling. She wasn't going anywhere any time soon, so there would be plenty of time for indulging.

"There will be ten, slave. Count them off."

And she began. First one pale cheek, and then the other. Over and over Dani swung the wooden paddle, connecting with Mike's ass with a sound *thwack*. As instructed Mike counted, and with each smack his voice grew raspier, huskier. When they reached ten both of them were breathing harsh, and a sheen of perspiration glistened on their flesh.

Dani's arousal was flying at breakneck speeds. Her hormones racing like an out of control locomotive. When Mike glanced over his shoulder at her, she was powerless to stop the shudder coursing through her that the glint in his eyes invoked.

"Thank you, my Mistress," he said.

"T-to the cross," she stammered.

Mike released his hold on the grips and stepped back from the post. Dani couldn't tear her eyes away from his reddened ass cheeks as he crossed the room toward the cross. With his back against the center support Mike bent over and wrapped the Velcro straps around his ankles. When he again stood he studied Dani with such intensity she felt herself waver.

"There's a step stool behind the door," he said. He must have read the confusion on her face because he added, "You'll need it to be tall enough to secure my wrists."

"Right," she said. After retrieving the stool and setting it beside him, she climbed up and fastened the straps around Mike's wrists.

A soft groan rumbled in his chest when her breast brushed along his side as she leaned in to fasten the restraints. The subtleness of his cologne mixed with a teasing muskiness assailed her senses when she inhaled a deep breath. Dani glanced over her raised arm and stifled a gasp. His eyes sparkled with mischief, and his full lips were now wet after running his tongue over them. Mike leaned over as if he would kiss her.

A voice in the back of her mind reminded her to regain control. Before his kissable lips touched hers, Dani reluctantly backed away. *We have all night.*

Stepping off the stool, she returned it to its place behind the door, and set out seeking a new implement. As she sashayed across the room Dani was sure to add a little more sway to her hips. She knew she'd succeeded in her visual seduction when a low, strangled groan carried to her ears.

From the selection of toys and tools Dani decided on a flogger. Long supple strips of leather dangled from one end, and polished aluminum decorated the other as a handle. The leather was soft as she threaded her fingers through the many ribbons. This implement wouldn't hurt as it danced across Mike's skin. It would create a more erotic sensation, like dozens of gentle fingers tickling his damp flesh.

After a couple of test swats against her hand, Dani turned her attention back to the restrained, naked man in the middle of the room. His nude body was a work of art, there was no question. The hunger in his eyes sent her heart thumping erratically inside her chest. At no time since disrobing had his erection weakened. His ability to sustain one for so long made her wet. Mike was who she was missing in her life. Who she needed to complete her.

Would Mike want that as well? Or was this simply a game to him?

Perhaps following their playtime they could sit down and talk about the possibility of a future together. Right now, she had a flogging to mete out.

"Have you ever been flogged?"

"No, Mistress."

"I've chosen this one specifically because of the suppleness of the leather," she explained.

"I trust you, my Mistress," Mike said in a tone that sent a chill rushing through her.

She shivered.

Before she began Dani stroked a hand over the hills and valleys of Mike chest and abdomen. The muscles rippled under her exploration. Her body ached to be caressed by Mike's large, strong hands. She wanted to feel his hands exploring her curves, his fingers coaxing out her deepest secrets. What would his lips feel like pressed against her flesh, or suckling her nipples?

Dani took a single step back, lifting the flogger, and with a flick of her wrist landed her first strike. Mike's skin danced, but his body remained still. She glanced up to look into his eyes, and he hitched his chin in silent challenge. In an effort to bring her arousal under control, she inhaled a deep breath. Again the leather straps sailed through the air to connect with Mike's frame.

Over and over she wielded the flogger, striking Mike's arms, legs, and washboard tummy. She continued to alter the force with which she swung the implement. A softer flick created a different sensation than a firmer one.

The entire time Mike's eyes held hers. Fire raged in his gaze. His breath was expelled in harsh pants as she persisted. She lost track of the passage of time. Stepping back to catch her breath, she dropped her eyes. When they settled on Mike's groin, her arousal took over.

Delicious droplets of pre-cum leaked from the slit at the end of his engorged cock. The flogger in her left hand fell to the floor with a *thud*, and she dropped to her knees before him. Unable to resist any longer, Dani leaned forward and licked the milky colored substance from the head of his shaft. The muskiness of his arousal whirled under her nose, further stimulating her already raging libido.

A soft moan was murmured from above. She cupped the taut sac dangling beneath the cock her mouth teased. Around the crown her tongue swirled in languid strokes until Mike's hips began to move with eagerness. There was no turning back. When she closed her lips over the broad crest his big body wavered. Her lips caressed the length of his shaft, her tongue gliding along the pulsing vein underside. The taste of him on her tongue was enough to send her body into orbit.

The combination of power and masculinity, mixed with a hint of vulnerability, set her body ablaze. Carnality swam in her veins, making her mind fuzzy.

Against her mouth Mike's hips thrust with growing urgency. Upon her tongue she tasted the tell-tale sign he was close. His flavor was like nothing she'd ever before sampled, and Dani knew this one night would never be enough.

She drew his cock deeper into her mouth. Faster she stroked him with her lips and tongue, every so often dragging her teeth along his iron-hard flesh. Higher her own arousal climbed until she teetered on the precipice of orgasm. With reluctance she released Mike's shaft to sit back on her heels. Using her hands, she balanced herself against his thighs.

"Jesus, don't stop." She barely heard Mike's strangled whisper through her ragged breaths. Try as she might, she was losing the ability to bring her fevered body back under control.

For speaking without permission he should be punished, but Dani didn't believe her legs would hold her up long enough to mete one out. If she hadn't stopped when she did, she for certain would have come right then and there. That wasn't what she wanted for her first time with Mike. She wanted him inside her. Thrusting, stroking, claiming her, if just for this one night.

Silent seconds between them stretched into minutes. Once she was sure her legs could sustain her weight, Dani stood. The scent of her excitement wafted up between them. If she could smell it, she was certain Mike could as well.

She met Mike's hungry gaze and arousal soared once again. With fiery need he held her attention. Desire, animalistic lust, burned in his dark eyes. The flare of his nostrils as he inhaled deeply threatened to do her in.

"What will you do now, my Mistress?" he asked. A glint of challenge flickered in his eyes, as if he sensed her desperation to jump him despite being restrained to the cross.

Afraid her voice would fail her, without a word Dani backed away while holding his heated gaze. Reaching up she held the clasp of her front closure of her bra and gave a twist, releasing her breasts from their lacy restraint. Mike's eyes widened with heightened interest. Turning her back, she bent at the waist and slid her panties over the curves of her buttocks and down her legs, giving him an unobstructed view of her wet slit. His tortured groan brought a smile to her lips. With a flirty grin over her shoulder, Dani walked to the table beside the bench and studied the variety of toys laid across the surface.

Picking up a life-like pink dildo, she turned back to face Mike, showing him her find. His cock was hard, the crown an angry red and leaking. The muscles in his upper body tensed as he tugged on the restraints holding his wrists.

"Now you will watch me pleasure myself, slave," she said.

Dani walked over and sat on the edge of the spanking bench a few feet away. His eyes bore into her, watching every move. Bringing the dildo up to her mouth she flicked her tongue out and over the tip of the firm rubber toy. Mike groaned from his spot on the cross, and began rocking his hips. Continuing her oral assault on the dildo, Dani shut her eyes and moaned aloud, closing her lips around the replica cock. Hollowing her cheeks, she sucked the toy deep before pulling it from her mouth and once again laving it with her wet tongue. Spreading her legs, she brought her right hand up to cup her breast. Tugging at her tight nipple earned her a strangled grunt and a hip thrust from the man staring at her.

* * * *

Slowly, Dani dragged the eight-inch dildo down her neck, between her breasts, along her belly, to stop just above her shaven pussy. She used her right hand to spread her plump folds open wide, to

[258]

reveal the swollen nub hidden within. With his eyes glued on her wet, exposed cunt, Dani slid the toy lower to tease the seeping opening. Pushing the dildo inside, she tossed her head back, thrusting her tits toward Mike in offering. Once six inches of the toy vanished she sighed, then withdrew it. While her left hand continued to work the toy in and out of her pussy, the fingers of her right began to rub and pluck at her clit.

"Mmm," she whimpered.

Mike eyes were focused on the woman before him, fucking herself with a fake cock when she was more than welcome to the one he was sporting, not more than four feet away. Christ, the aroma of her arousal had been driving him insane. He knew she'd been close to coming several times as her musky scent filled the room. Little did she know, he was about to make her suffer as she'd made him since arriving in his suite. Hell, for the past month.

The dildo glistened with her juice as she pulled it from her pussy. Reading the expression on her beautiful face, her eyes squeezed closed, biting her lower lip, Mike knew she was climbing for orgasm. She would not reach it without his help.

Or his permission.

A forceful tug snapped the Velcro around his wrists. The rendering of the straps caused Dani's eyes to shoot open and her hands to cease their ministrations. The gaping look of surprise she stared back at him with made him chuckle. When she saw he was free, she leapt to her feet and dropped the dildo to the floor with a *thud*. He took a step toward her, and she sidestepped around the bench, putting a few feet between them.

"Don't you move a muscle, my Mistress," he said.

"Your ankles. Your wrists," she gasped, wide eyed.

"You should have checked to be sure your slave obeyed your direction, Mistress."

"But…"

Mike continued to stalk toward her.

"No buts, my pretty little slave. Your presence in this club has taunted me for over a month. Actually, thirty-five days to be exact," he declared. "You invade my dreams, my thoughts, and I can't think straight when a vision of your curvaceous body flashes in my mind. This, for the record, is all the fucking time."

A feminine gasp slipped past her parted lips.

"To add to my pleasurable agony, I've been enjoying the smell of your pussy for close to an hour. Now, I'm going to taste you."

Her eyes grew as big as saucers, flickering with her escalating arousal. The rise and fall of her breasts as she labored for breath stimulated him even more. The stunned look on her face seconds before had now transformed to one of pure excitement.

"I'm the Mistress," she muttered with wavering confidence.

The sudden change in her body language confirmed he'd knocked her off balance. Control had been granted to Dani long enough. Mike now intended to take what was his. He would stake his claim.

"The hell you are," he growled.

Like a predator after his prey, Mike stalked forward. Dani countered him step for step as he backed her toward the wall. She had to tilt her head back to look up at him. Desire and need reflected back at him in her eyes. His large hands gripped her waist, and effortlessly Mike lifted her frame. Pressing her back against the wall, leveling her pussy with his face, the Dominant in him emerged.

"Legs over my shoulders," he ordered.

Her uttered gasp of protest made him smile. "Mike, please."

"Don't make me repeat myself, Danielle," his tone cautioned.

With her hands clutching his biceps, Dani lifted her legs over his shoulders. Her body trembled once she settled.

"Good girl," he praised, and moved his face close to inhale her scent.

Dani's muskiness washed over Mike. He was in heaven. The aroma of her arousal, a life-giving aphrodisiac he would never again be able to live without.

"Since the moment I laid eyes on you, you've consumed me. Besides sinking myself inside you, I want to know everything about you. Like your birthday—"

"April sixth."

"Favorite color?"

"Yellow."

"Turn on?"

"What?"

"We have an afternoon alone together. What do we do?"

"After a romantic picnic by the lake," she first panted, and then growled, "we do the wild thing in the backseat of your car!"

"Food?"

"My mom's apple pie. She makes it with caramel."

"Nice. I now have a sudden need to cover your entire body in caramel and lick you clean. Your biggest disappointment?"

"Not being with you before this minute."

"Jesus, baby."

Mike knew that after he tasted her there would never be anyone else again, as long as he lived, who would satisfy him sexually. Would Dani be interested in entertaining the possibility of something more? He hoped so, but for now, all that mattered was for the two of them to come together, to fulfill the deep physical and emotional need they both clearly shared.

"Mike," she whispered. "W-what are you going to do?"

"Everything I want. Now open yourself to me," Mike commanded in a hoarse voice. "I want to see how beautiful your sweet smelling pussy is."

Without hesitation Dani released her grip on his arms and reached between her legs. Mike's eyes centered on the smooth, shaven lips inches from his face, as Dani used her slender fingers to spread her folds. A husky moan came from above him, and her body shuddered against the wall.

"Wider, baby."

As she did, Mike leaned forward and slid the flat of his tongue along her opening to the tip of her clit. Closing his lips around the pink nub, he suckled lightly before slipping his tongue up inside her. Farther he probed, savoring the unique flavor of her. Despite the painful throb between his legs needing to be buried deep inside Dani's body, Mike could die a happy man at having just tasted her.

Dani's hips began to wiggle, and she tried to move even closer to his feasting mouth. With a gentle nip to her inner right thigh, Dani's movement froze. He hadn't bit her enough to cause her intense pain, but she would bear his mark.

"Be still, my slave. I'm far from having my fill of you," Mike growled against her mound. With another flick of his tongue against her clit, Dani cried out. "And don't even think about coming without my permission, baby."

"But, Mike," she sobbed. "I'm so close now."

"Well, I'm not done, so you're going to have to hold it."

Ignoring her protests, Mike went back to devouring Dani's pussy. Her scent and taste clouded his rational thought. He couldn't get enough of her. The sounds of her ragged breath as she fought to control the climb to release made his balls tighten under his shaft.

Beneath his hands, her body trembled, her skin dampening at an alarming rate, and Dani gasped out incoherent words.

"M—M—Mi…" he heard, and knew he'd better allow her a brief reprieve.

"Thirty seconds, baby," he told her, after pulling away. "That's how long you have to get yourself under control."

The fiery look in her eyes had Mike near shooting his load all over the wall in front of him. The need to be brought to release made her dark brown orbs sparkle. The desire not to let him down flickered bright. As the seconds ticked by Dani struggled to draw breath. Deeply she would inhale, and shudder on exhale.

Mike lifted his head and lowered her body enough to drag his tongue across one peaked nipple before the other. The twin berries strained, growing a deeper shade of pink as they beckoned another wet caress. Closing his lips around the tip of her right breast, Mike drew the tight peak into his mouth. Rolling his tongue over the bud, his teeth nipped the puckered flesh, bringing a sharp cry from the depths of Dani's chest. When her fingers fisted in his hair, holding his head in place, Mike ceased his torture.

"Keep your pussy open for me, slave girl," he ordered, and tightened his grip on her waist. "I want to savor the scent of you while I enjoy your beautiful tits."

Dani unthreaded her fingers from Mike's curls and again reached between her legs.

"Good girl," he praised, and drew her left nipple into his mouth and suckled the peak hard.

When her breath grew ragged, he pulled away from her breast as he held her gaze. She was so close to climax he could smell her arousal growing muskier.

"You still cannot come without my permission," he reminded her before nipping at the flesh around her right breast.

"Mike—"

"Master," he corrected.

"Master," she repeated in a raspy voice, without hesitating. "Master, please. I need to come."

The sound of her husky voice calling him 'Master' was nearly enough to push Mike over the edge.

"I don't think so," he said, and dipped his head between her thighs again. "You've teased me for weeks, baby. I'm taking a few more minutes."

For several moments Mike's tongue continued to lap and his lips pluck at her swollen clit. Her sensual moans of pleasure fed his need. He pushed her sexual desire higher, ignoring her mewling protests, until she fell silent, and her body quivered uncontrollably against the wall where he still held her.

Mike glanced up. Dani's top teeth were sunk into her lower lip, and her eyes were squeezed shut. Perspiration trickled down her heated flesh in rivulets.

"Dani?" Mike questioned in a whisper.

"I d-didn't," she stammered and gasped for air. "I...didn't, Mike—Master," she quickly corrected herself. "I s-swear."

Mike knew he'd pushed her pretty hard, and it thrilled him that she had fought off her orgasm to please him.

"I know, baby," he said in an assuring tone. "Are you all right?"

She gave a slight nod and moaned as a tremor moved through her.

"Good girl, Dani," Mike praised in a soft voice. "Hold it for me. I promise your reward will be worth the wait."

"I'm on fire, Mike," she said in a strangled cry.

Heavy perspiration covered Dani's flesh. Her brunette waves a sexy, tousled mess, with strands clinging to her cheeks and neck. Through half-closed eyelids she met his gaze. She caught her breath, and Mike knew it was in reaction to the hunger she'd seen in his eyes.

"I know you are, my honey." He chuckled low. "That's the idea.

[265]

Now you know what you do to me."

A seductive grin curled Dani's lips. "Really?" she asked, hesitant curiosity heavy in her voice.

Mike nodded. Though Dani was light as a feather, his arms were feeling the tension of holding her in the position against the wall for the past twenty minutes.

"I set your body on fire?"

"Yeah, you do. Come on, slide your legs down, baby," he told her. When she did, Mike lowered her until her feet settled on the floor. "Under your touch, I lose all conscious thought," he admitted, and continued to hold her around the waist until the circulation returned to her feet and toes.

Mike's cock pressed against Dani's belly as he held her. Once again her fingers dug into his forearms as she sought balance.

"Are you ready to continue, slave?"

"If you stop now I'll kill you," she replied.

Mike bent down to scoop Dani up in his arms. She buried her face into the crook of his neck, nuzzling, kissing, and nipping his throat. He carried her across the playroom and through the door to his bedroom.

In the middle of his bed he laid her and reached for the nightstand. From the drawer he gathered the box of condoms he'd purchased earlier in the day and a tube of lubricant.

"Let me," she offered after watching him fumble with the box.

His anxiousness to be inside her was affecting his fine motor skills. He prayed he'd be able to exercise some finesse.

She pulled a ream of rubbers from the box, and ripped one off at the perforation. Mike noticed Dani's hands were shaking just as his were. For a moment he questioned if she was nervous from anticipation and excitement, as he was, or was she worried because of his size that he'd hurt her. His query was extinguished when she ripped open the foil packet with her teeth, with a savagery to rival a lioness eating her prey.

Mike pushed his hips forward as she reached to roll the rubber onto his dick, her touch gentle and sure. When her teeth bit into her lower lip Mike's balls threatened to burst. Popping the cap on the lube, he squeezed a glob into his hand and stroked his length. When he reached to smear some on Dani's pussy she chuckled.

"I'm already pretty wet," she told him.

"Baby, I'm not bragging, but my cock is a hell of a lot bigger than that dildo you were toying with. I want in you so fucking bad, I'm afraid I might hurt you. I don't want to do that." He proceeded to ensure Dani was prepared to take every fat inch of him.

After wiping his hand on a towel he'd left on the foot of the bed for just this instance, he settled himself between Dani's splayed thighs. His large body completely covered her smaller one. He feared he'd squish her if he wasn't careful.

"Please, Mike," she pleaded. "We've waited long enough."

Mike grabbed his cock in his hand and pushed his hips forward until the head of it slipped inside her slick entrance. Despite the generousness of the clear jelly, he met resistance. Several times he pulled back at the thought of causing her pain. His gut ached at the thought. He didn't want to hurt her, just love her.

Sweat popped out of his pores as he restrained himself. The need to thrust deep was great, but her comfort more important. If it took him all night to enter her tight sheath, then so be it. Her hips thrust upward, pulling him in a bit at a time.

"Mike, please," she repeated.

He gained another inch before her body stiffened. Her muscles pulsed and clenched around him, fighting against his advances. He glanced down and grimaced. Hell, he'd only managed to slide half his prick inside her. This just might kill him. Down the length of his back her delicate fingers gently caressed, until she came to his ass. After cupping the cheeks, she dug her nails into his flesh. Instinct made him thrust forward to ease the splinters of pain she created.

"I don't want to hurt you," he growled when he realized her motivation.

"You won't hurt me, damn it. Now give me what I want."

This time when she dug into his ass she thrust her hips up, her body swallowing the last few inches of his cock. The seam of her buttocks cradled his sac as he pressed against her. Her cunt fought his intrusion, yet she held him tight. Mike doubted he could pull away if his life depended on it.

Mike watched as a multitude of expressions crossed her face. Perspiration peppered her upper lip and forehead. Beneath him her body trembled. When her lower lip began to quiver Mike was yanked back to reality.

"You're in pain," he ground out.

Her eyelids fluttered open, and she smiled. "Only in the most fabulous way," she purred.

A moment passed while he absorbed her words. He had to have caused her intense discomfort. He'd just shoved his giant dick inside her tight, unyielding pussy, and she was smiling at him?

This wasn't how it was supposed to be. He'd wanted their first time to be a loving and tender experience, despite his raging hormones. The BDSM stuff was for fun, and when she'd gotten her fill of "punishing" him, it would be him who showed her just how gentle he could be.

He wished he could turn back the clock, if only for a few minutes.

"What did I say about you stopping, Master?" Dani's fingertips began dancing along the flesh of his back.

Mike searched her face for something, anything, to hint that she wasn't just saying what he wanted to hear, that she didn't truly want him to pull out. All he saw was desire and need in her eyes. Her smile widened, and she wiggled her hips as much as she could with his weight pressed onto her.

"As you wish, my Mistress," he said, and then captured her mouth with his.

Beneath him her body lay pinned, yet her tongue fought his to dominate their oral embrace. Between her legs he stroked a demanding, confident rhythm. Within moments her pussy tightened around him, pulling, insistent. She was close, but seemed unwilling to take the leap alone. Dani wrapped her legs around his back, hooking her ankles as best she could. Against his chest her hands pressed as if providing her leverage as he pushed her across the bed with every thrust of his hips.

[269]

"Now. Please," she begged and ordered at the same time.

"Yes, my baby, now."

CHAPTER 5

"Hey, Mike," Dani called from his kitchenette the following morning. "We're out of juice, milk, wine, even beer. Cleaned you right out of all liquids."

In more ways than one, he mused.

"I'll run downstairs and grab a couple bottles of water," he announced, joining her and scooping her up in his arms.

Dani squealed, wrapping her arms around his neck. "You're such a brute," she teased, nuzzling his throat.

He sauntered across the suite, and when he crossed the threshold of the bedroom, he tossed her onto the middle of his bed.

"Wee," Dani cheered as her body sailed through the air.

"I'll be five minutes, babe," he said, his eyes taking in every curvaceous inch of her. God, he was in love. "You'd better be sprawled across my bed, naked, when I get back."

"Or what?" A sassy smirk curled her lips as she got up on her hands and knees.

"I'll paddle your ass," he replied.

"Ooo, doesn't that sound like fun."

Mike bent over and dropped a kiss on her full lips. "Be right back."

"I'll be waiting."

Pulling the door to his suite closed, Mike found himself grinning ear to ear. He'd never been so happy in his life. He'd met his sexual match in Dani, and now he needed to convince her there could be more to a life with him than earth-shattering sex. Every day for the rest of his life he wanted to wake up next to her. Holding her snug against his chest is how he wanted to fall asleep each and every night.

As Mike neared the landing, thumping on the back staff entrance door gained his attention.

"Who the hell is that so early in the damn morning?" He glanced at the clock beside the door and grinned. It was eleven-thirty. "Guess it's not so early after all."

The knocking became louder, more insistent. No one who should be knocking would be in for another couple of hours.

"Okay, okay, I'm coming. Christ," Mike called out. "What the hell is your problem?" he growled when he swung the heavy steel door open.

Standing before him wearing a finely tailored suit stood the state's senator. Mike recognized him immediately: he was always in the news. Four bodyguards accompanied him, two standing on each side. Mike was pretty sure the slight bulges under their jackets were an indication they were packing heat.

"It's about fucking time," the man snapped, pushing his way past Mike.

"Can I help you with something?" Mike asked, and followed him up the hall toward the bar.

"Where is she?" the senator asked.

"Where's who?" Mike countered.

"My daughter. I know she's here."

Mike's mind raced. "Sir?"

"Megan Washington, you imbecile. Where is she?"

Mike breathed a sigh of relief, thankful Dani's father hadn't come knocking.

* * * *

Tense minutes passed as the senator berated Mike, and the club as a whole, while the men accompanying him remained silent. It was evident the situation was getting out of hand, and considering the odds of five to one weren't in Mike's favor he decided to call in reinforcements.

Inside the bar area, Mike picked up the phone and dialed Troy's cellphone.

"Hey, Mike."

"Really sorry to bother you, Troy."

"No, no, it's all right," Troy said. "What's up?"

"We've got a situation." Mike ran his fingers through his hair. "Listen pal, as much as I hate to interrupt your morning, I think you'd better come down here."

"Who's doing all the yelling?"

"Megan's old man. Buddy, I've got a very unhappy senator on my hands."

"Are you serious?"

"Oh, yeah. He's refusing to leave, and threatening to take this place down brick by brick until he gets his hands on his daughter."

"I'm on my way. Give me a few minutes."

True to his word, a few minutes later the door to the private suites opened and Troy and Ransom, along with Megan, strolled in. Though security was Mike's position, Troy was the club manager, and calm negotiations were his field of expertise.

"Senator, I'm going to have to ask you to lower your voice, please," Troy said.

"If you think for one minute that you're going to tell me what to do, young man, you're out of your fucking mind. And *you*..." The senator pointed at Megan. "How dare you sully my reputation in this manner? You selfish, spoiled brat."

"What exactly is it that *our* Megan has done to 'sully your reputation,' sir?" Troy asked.

Mike always admired how calm Troy could remain in any situation.

"What the hell were you thinking coming into a place like this? The reporter who shot this photo," he yelled as he held a newspaper over his head, "said he sat out front for hours, and you didn't come out. Do you know how many reporters are parked out front of this shit hole right now?"

"And?" Troy asked.

"And it sure as shit looks like she spent the night! Look at you! Did you spend all fucking night lying on your back with your God damned legs in the air?"

"That'll be enough of that," Troy snarled. "You will not speak to Megan that way."

Senator Washington gave Troy a look of utter disdain. "For Crissakes girl, what the hell did you do here all night?"

"That isn't any of your business, Senator," Ransom said calmly.

The senator turned his angry gaze on his daughter. A moment later, his face turned bright red. "You let these two fuck you, didn't you? Do you have any idea how this is going to affect *me* once this gets out? You're no better than a slut. You're just a common *whore*."

"Dad," Megan gasped.

"Why you son of a bitch," Ransom exploded. Megan placed a hand on his chest, stopping him from advancing on her father.

When Mike would have joined Ransom, the look in Megan's eyes pulled him up short. Sad as it seemed, it was clear outbursts like the one they were witnessing weren't new to her.

Instead of taking a step forward to protect the senator, the bodyguards took a step back. Megan released Troy's hand and stepped toward her father. Troy and Ransom stayed close.

"Dad, please, calm down—"

"You are a disgrace. A huge disappointment. To think I wasted my sperm creating you."

Megan's body stiffened, all color draining from her face. The hurt in her eyes made Mike's blood boil. No, she wasn't his woman, but Jesus Christ, what sort of man said something like that to his own daughter? When Mike joined Dani back in his suite he would insist they meet each other's parents and get their relationship out in the open.

"Now you get your worthless ass out the back fucking door, and into my limo," Megan's father ordered. "We'll join my team doing damage control from home."

The seconds ticked by. Anger, frustration and confusion radiated off Megan. Mike could see Troy and Ransom were doing their best to keep it together.

"We meant what we said, honey," Troy said, his eyes glued on Megan's dad. "You don't have to go anywhere."

"Your home is right here with us, baby," Ransom added.

After several tense moments, Megan shook her head. "No, Dad. I'm not going anywhere."

"Don't you dare back talk me, you hussy." The senator attempted to smack Megan with the newspaper in his hand.

Troy pulled Megan to him. Without argument, she placed herself behind his body. Ransom grabbed the senator's wrist in mid-air.

"Whoa, old man," Ransom growled. As he pulled the senator's hand down, the man winced in pain.

"Are you four baboons going to do something?" Senator Washington snarled at the bodyguards.

The man standing on his immediate left lifted his chin. "I don't think so, sir. These fellows have things well in hand."

"You were hired to protect *me*," the senator roared. "And I expect you to do your job, asshole. Arrest them. Do something!"

"I don't know who the hell you think you are, but I'm not about to offer assistance to a political figure, or any man for that matter, who attempts to hit his daughter, and speaks to her like you just have."

"Why you bastard. You are fired!"

"Since you don't pay my wages, sir, that's not your call," the man pointed out, his tone completely calm. "But I'm more than happy to put in for reassignment."

"Now, Senator," Troy said. "You will leave without further incident."

"I'm not going anywhere without my daughter."

The door to the private corridor opened, and feminine giggling drew the attention of the group. Max Renfrew entered with Natalie on his arm. He wore only a pair of boxer shorts, while she was dressed in one of Max's t-shirts.

"I'm sorry. I wasn't expecting anyone to be down yet." Max surveyed the situation, and his eyes narrowed with concern. "What's going on here?"

"Natalie?" Megan was clearly surprised to see her friend.

"Meg?" Natalie replied.

"The senator was just leaving," Troy informed Max.

"The hell I am."

"Senator Washington!" Natalie gasped. She stepped behind Max, tugging at the hem of the t-shirt.

"Well, seeing *you* here does not surprise me," the senator said. "What the hell have you gotten my daughter into?"

"Now you wait just a minute, sir." Max took a step forward. "Senator, you will leave my establishment now, or I'll be placing a call to the police and filing a harassment suit."

"Max? You... You own this club?" Megan asked.

Max nodded in her direction as the back door opened again. This time Dani's voice stopped everyone cold.

"Where's my super hunky slave boy at? Yoohoo, Mikey, baby. Your Mistress wants to *plaaayyy*."

When she came into view, several startled gasps and a couple of strangled groans were heard. One was his own. Dani wore a pair of tiny black panties and a black leather corset with holes in the center of the breast cups that left her rosy-tipped nipples completely exposed. In her right hand she held a riding crop.

That's my girl.

"What the hell is going on?" she asked calmly. Her eyes settled on Mike. "I thought you came down here to grab us some water?"

As his eyes savored her scantily clad form, Mike shrugged. "Something came up." He jerked his thumb toward the others in the room.

"I should have known you and the other tart were behind this," Megan's father said.

"Hey, who are you calling a tart?" Natalie said, stepping out from behind Max.

Dani tipped her head coyly, a sly smile curling her lips. "Nice to see you here without your usual disguise, Senator."

Whoa! Didn't see that coming.

Judging from the stunned expressions on everyone else's face, they hadn't expected it either.

The senator turned white as a sheet. "Why you smug little

trollop!"

Mike was thankful Troy stepped in, because he himself was seeing red. The only thing he wanted to do was rip the senator's throat out. Despite being equally as pissed, Troy would be more rational.

"This meeting is over." Troy turned to Megan. "Sweetheart, you take Natalie and Dani up to *our* suite. *Yours*, Ransom and my home."

"Troy," she whispered.

"*Our* home," he repeated. Troy brushed his thumb across Megan's cheek to wipe away a single tear trickling down. "We will see your father and his escorts out, then we will be right up."

Megan nodded.

Mike found himself wondering if Dani would be as ready to accept a life with him.

"I love you, Megan." Troy spoke a little louder than necessary, and Mike assumed it was to ensure that everyone in the room heard his words. "Now, go."

As she turned, Ransom grabbed her arms and spun her around to face him. Holding the angry gaze of her father a moment longer, Ransom lowered his mouth and kissed her long and hard.

The senator took a step forward, but the bodyguard on his right stopped him. "Don't even think about it," the man said.

Ransom pulled away and looked down at Megan. "I love you too, baby." Urging Megan to the door leading to the private suite, Ransom released her.

Once the door had closed behind the women, Troy, Ransom, Mike and Max advanced. Two of the bodyguards were young, very young,

[279]

and clearly lacking experience. They had remained silent during the entire confrontation and now appeared to be sizing up the competition. With effort Mike contained a snicker of amusement as he read their deduction.

Of the four men, Max was the smallest in stature. Yet despite being clad in only a pair of silk boxers, his six-one, two-hundred-fifteen pound presence was threatening. Ransom and Troy were close in height and stature, standing around six-three, each weighing close to two-hundred-thirty pounds. Then there was Mike, himself. He was the largest, standing six-five and tipping the scales at around two-hundred-seventy-five pounds.

"We are done here, gentlemen," Troy said. "Senator or not, and at this moment I don't give a flying fuck that you're Megan's old man, you have ten seconds to get the hell out of this club."

"I'm not leaving my daughter with you two miscreants, in this dump that promotes your dysfunctional way of life."

"Get him out, *now*," Troy said. There was no mistaking the warning in his tone.

"Senator," the man to his right spoke. "Sir, my men and I are leaving, with or without you." When the senator didn't move, the bodyguard prompted again. "Sir, last warning. Let's go."

"I am *not* finished with you," the senator threatened.

"Looking forward to seeing you again, Senator," Troy replied.

The bodyguards aided the still fighting and cursing senator down the corridor and out the back door.

After throwing the double deadbolt, Max turned back toward the

[280]

three men. "Well, that was rather unpleasant for first thing in the morning," he said.

"What happened? How'd he get in?" Troy asked.

"I came downstairs, and somebody was pounding on the door so hard I thought they were going to break it down," Mike admitted, as the men started climbing the stairs. "When I opened the door he pushed past me. Sorry to spoil your morning, Troy. I didn't think it would be a good idea to get physical, at least not until every attempt had been made to reason with him, but the guy wouldn't listen. With your skill at reasoning with people I knew you'd bring diplomacy to the situation."

"No problem, big man," Troy said. "The old fellow's got issues, and nobody needs to put up with that sort of bullshit."

* * * *

The door to Troy and Ransom's suite opened, and all four men entered.

"Well?" Megan asked as Ransom approached and wrapped his arms around her.

"Let's just say I doubt the senator will be sending the club a Christmas card this year." Ransom dropped a kiss on the top of her head. "You okay?"

"I'll be fine. I'm used to his tirades."

"You sure you're all right, Megan?" Max asked.

Mike watched Megan nod, but she remained silent. The poor woman looked beyond embarrassed. Humiliated would be more accurate. Mike felt for her.

"Okay, well, now that that unpleasantness is concluded, the group of us has reservations at The Cove for brunch. A limo will be here in an hour to pick us up," Max announced as he crossed the room toward Natalie.

"That's nice." Natalie accepted his hand, and he pulled her to her feet. "What's the occasion?"

"We're celebrating the first day of the rest of our lives," Max replied. "Come on, move that sweet ass, Nat. I'd like to make love to you before we leave."

"Ahh, damn! An hour doesn't give me nearly enough time to punish my Mikey," Dani said with a sassy grin as Mike approached her. "That's all right, we'll do a quickie now, and then a longie when we get back."

"Sounds good to me, babe." Mike picked Dani up and tossed her over his shoulder. Mike knew he'd never want to be anywhere else, ever again.

* * * *

After they'd both reached climax Dani lay sprawled across Mike's body, her head resting on his chest.

"That was great," he said, running his fingers through her hair.

"Mmm-mmm," she purred in agreement.

Mike glanced at the clock on the table beside his bed. "We better get ready. The limo will be here in fifteen minutes."

"Think Max will mind if we skip brunch?" Dani asked, and ran a fingertip over his erect nipple.

"Yeah, he might. Come on, we need sustenance and there's nothing around here for us to eat."

"Oh, fine," she groused and wiggled off him.

"Remember, we've got a longie to look forward to when we get back."

"That's right," she purred, stroking her hand along his abdomen.

After a very quick shower, they stood in Mike's bedroom getting dressed. He watched Dani as she studied the red miniskirt she'd worn the night before, indecision evident in her expression. When she looked over at him, he smiled.

"I have something for you." He turned and walked to his closet.

"For me?"

Mike pulled a clothing bag from his closet and reached for the zipper. "Brunch wasn't a surprise for us guys. It was part of Max's master plan. But I knew it would be for you, and remembering your attire when you came to the club for your sessions..." he said, enjoying the blush tinting her cheeks as he reminded her of her state of undress during her training. "Anyhow, I thought you might like this."

With the zipper lowered, Mike slid the plastic bag over the hanger, revealing a floral print sundress. Dani's face lit up.

"There were lots of colors, but I liked the yellow the best," he said. "Not bad considering I only found out last night it's your favorite color."

"It's beautiful, Mike," she said, and crossed the floor toward him. She rose to her tiptoes, and he dipped his head to press a kiss against her lips.

"Thank you," she added, taking the dress off the hanger. After unzipping it and slipping it over her head, she turned her back to him, lifting her long, dark curls out of the way.

Mike placed a kiss between her shoulder blades as he zipped the dress closed.

"Well?" she asked, spinning in a circle before him. "What do you think?"

"I think I am the luckiest man alive," he replied. "You're gorgeous."

"Mike," she uttered tentatively.

"Yeah, baby?"

"What happens now?"

"We go to brunch. Our hour's up."

"No, what happens after brunch?"

"We come back here and make love until we're spent."

Her top teeth sunk into her lower lip. "And after that?"

Mike studied Dani for several moments in silence. He knew it was impulsive, but it was now or never. He had to tell her how he was feeling, and prayed she felt the same way.

"Move in with me," he requested. "And we'll take it from there."

Dani blinked several times. His statement caught her unawares. "I have a cat. Is there room in your heart for Lady Godiva?"

"Lady Godiva?"

"My cat."

"Oh, jeez, she sounds high maintenance," Mike groaned. A wide smile lifted his lips.

"She's a cat, of course she's high maintenance. Cats have staff you know, not owners."

"I don't know, baby," he said, fastening the buttons of his shirt. "I'm more of a goldfish sort of guy."

Her shoulders slumped. "Really?"

"Yeah," he replied, and grinned. "But if it means keeping you in my bed every night, I suppose I could learn to tolerate your cat."

A smile curled Dani's full, delicious lips. "Yeah?"

"I'm not promising anything where your cat is concerned," Mike said and opened his arms to her. "I like goldfish."

Dani stepped into his embrace, wrapping her arms around his body. "Then I'll get you one. Maybe two. And do you know why, Mike Ranger?"

"Why?"

"Because I've fallen for you. In a big way, big man."

Mike bent down and scooped her up in his arms.

"That's a good thing, baby. Because I fell for you the moment I first laid eyes on you. I've been waiting patiently for you to catch up."

ABOUT JENNIFER COLE

http://www.lyricalpress.com/jennifer_cole

By day, Jennifer Cole is a mild mannered administrative assistant in a bustling office. By night, she shuts out the world of reality and enters...the realm of erotic romance and fantasy. Living for an exhilarating plot and wickedly delicious sex scenes, there is nothing too outrageous or off limits for this slave to eroticism; in fact, the naughtier the encounter, the better.

* * * *

After reading a number of erotic romances I got the bright idea it might be fun to write one. Seems I possess a talent to tell a lascivious tale. Regardless of the steamy sexy stories I create, for me it's all about true love and happily-ever-after, or a reasonable facsimile—the guy must get the girl in the end.

On those rare occasions when I manage to steal some spare time, I read. When not sweating over the laptop tapping to keep up with my over-active imagination, I squeeze in running, cycling, trips to the gym and occasionally shoot pool. Above everything else, I cherish time spent with my family and friends.

Currently I make my home in a small city in South-western Ontario and just enjoy life.

A simple girl with simple indulgences, that's me. I listen to rock music, enjoy expensive cognac and oh, I've never met a cookie I didn't like!

Jennifer's Website:
http://www.freewebs.com/jennifericole/
Reader eMail:
jennifercole.author@gmail.com

About the Le Club d'Esclavage Series

Book I: *At the Dungeon Master's Hand*
Available in ebook from Lyrical Press, Inc.
Book II: *A Toy for Two*
Available in ebook from Lyrical Press, Inc.
Book III: *Yes, My Mistress*
Available in ebook from Lyrical Press, Inc.

Breinigsville, PA USA
28 September 2010
246299BV00001B/14/P